THE F

To Imogen

THE
FORGOTTEN
PALACE

I really hope you enjoy this book too!

AN ADVENTURE IN PRESADIA

God bless,

LUKE AYLEN

Luke Aylen

LION FICTION

Published by
Lion Hudson Limited
Wilkinson House, Jordan Hill Business Park
Banbury Road, Oxford OX2 8DR, England
www.lionhudson.com

ISBN 978 1 7826 4279 4
e-ISBN 978 1 7826 4280 0

First edition 2019

Cover image acknowledgments
Palace © Slava Gerj/Shutterstock
Eye © Refluo/Shutterstock

A catalogue record for this book is available from the British Library

Printed and bound in the UK, February 2019, LH26

CONTENTS

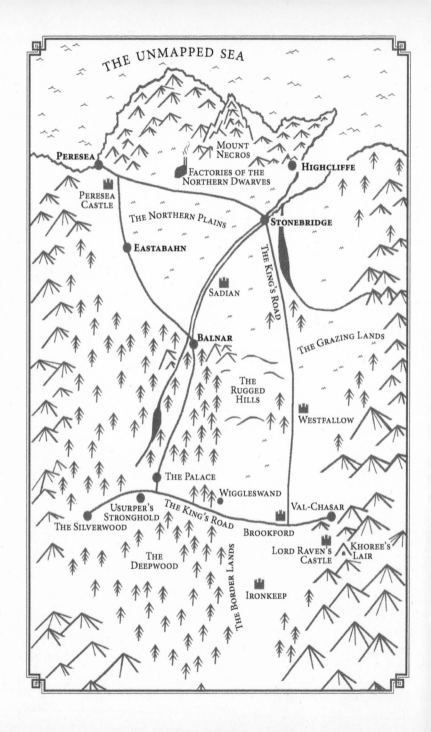

1

GLITTER AND DUST

"*Opal, over here!*" *Copper's voice echoed down the left-hand fork of the tunnel. "The sound is coming from down this passageway."*

Opal hurried after the distant glow of her husband's magma-worm lantern, holding her own lamp high. Again, she heard the strange whimpering sound. It was high-pitched and awoke inside her a feeling of longing, as though a fist were clenched around her heart.

What was making the sound? These tunnels were long abandoned. The densely cobwebbed entrance proved they were the first to venture down these passages in many, many years. Soot lay thick on the floor. The only tracks in the dust were their own and the little footprints of rats or cave crabs.

Cobwebs broke against her face as she neared the glow of her husband's lantern. The tunnel curved suddenly to avoid a glittering deposit of crystal-like material in the wall ahead. It was **majis-glatheras** *– king's glass – the strongest material the dwarves had ever found. It wasn't particularly rare, but no tools the dwarves possessed would cut through it, although once upon a time, supposedly, people had been able to work it. Legend said that the old king himself had been a master of crafting the beautiful mirrored crystals. Whatever the case, now the knowledge and tools were long gone. When the* *tunnels hit a particularly large deposit like this one, the miners were forced to chisel their way around it before carrying on.*

It sparkled in the lantern light in flashes of vibrant colour as Opal hurried past. Her husband was just around the bend, framed by glittering king's glass.

He was stooping over. The whimpering sound that had led them deep into the abandoned tunnels was coming from the bundle he was lifting carefully.

Opal stopped in her tracks as Copper straightened up.

"Great bronze beard of Boron, Opal, it's a baby! A little baby!" Tears glinted in his eyes. "Our prayers have been answered," he whispered, staring down in disbelief at the tiny face peering back at him.

⚜

"Is anyone there?"

The muffled cry sounded again.

Antimony was getting closer. His eyes scanned the tumbled-down remains of the freshly ruined castle for any sign of the survivor.

"I'm down here."

The voice came from Antimony's left.

He clambered over some smashed timbers and a large section of wall that, until only recently, would have stood upright. Now it blanketed the ruins like a strange cobbled road, bulging and breaking but still remarkably complete.

"Hello? I can hear you! Keep shouting. I'll find you," Antimony called.

To his surprise, the trapped voice started singing in a crisp and melodious voice. It was a silly tune, such as one might sing to a small child. In the desperate and harsh surroundings of the ruined castle it felt entirely out of place, but Antimony supposed it would be as effective as anything else. He turned toward the voice and picked his way between wood, stone, ash, and dust.

> *"There was a young dwarf from the hills,*
> *Who was scared, for the dark gave him chills.*
> *But his beard was so long*
> *That the people all thronged,*
> *And made him their Lord 'gainst his will."*

Antimony skidded across a precarious pile of huge bricks as he followed the sing-song voice. Perhaps the singing man's wits had cracked. Antimony had heard that could happen to people when they went through dreadful things. And what had happened here, in this castle, must have been pretty dreadful.

It had been Salt's idea to come back here. They had been heading home to the dwarfish city of Val-Chasar and the castle had been only a little off their route. Antimony and Salt both felt partly responsible for the damage that had been done here.

> *"They took the young dwarf to their mines,*
> *But he hated the dingy confines,*
> *So he lit up a lamp*
> *In the gloom and the damp,*
> *And it blazed out a glorious shine."*

How much could change in such a short space of time! At their last visit, only days ago, Lord Raven's castle had stood undamaged and proud, looking out over a valley of fields and woodland. It was unrecognizable now. Where once-elegant towers had soared beside mighty walls, there was heaped rubble. Where fields of crops had blanketed the valley, there was mud and rubbish and the smouldering remains of farms and houses.

"Now the dark and the light are not friends –
They hide from each other round bends.
In the deep dwarfish mines
They draw battle lines;
Light attacks where the darkness defends."

The castle and surrounding areas had fallen victim to a great battle; a battle that had been stirred up by the dwarves so they could make money selling weapons to both sides. Antimony had been there when the siege started. They had been selling a final shipment of supplies to the desperate defenders for a hefty profit. Desperate people paid desperate prices.

If it hadn't been for the bizarre meeting with a strange girl from a completely different world, Antimony would probably never have thought about the castle again.

"The young dwarf with light on his side
Realized that darkness would hide,
So his fear disappeared,
And by great Boron's beard,
He found courage from deep down inside."

Antimony squeezed through a half-collapsed doorway into the hollow shell of a destroyed tower. Was the voice coming from in here? Square walls still rose above him on all sides, but instead of sturdy ceiling timbers above his head, stormy clouds billowed in an angry sky, framed by the jagged edges of the broken tower. The floors of the tower had collapsed beneath the onslaught of the catapults and the weight of falling masonry, filling the basement with a mishmash of rubble, broken furniture and splintered floorboards.

"The young dwarf had come to see clear
That, though darkness oft stakes its claim here,
Goodness and light
Amidst darkness is bright,
So he shone out his light without fear."

The man's voice was very close now – just below him, in fact. Antimony peered down into the dusty shadows of the basement below him, searching for the poor soul trapped beneath the rubble. A glitter amid the filth and rubble caught his eye. Crouching to get a better view, he saw shattered shards of a mirror among the wreckage.

The shards flickered like a broken rainbow and reminded him again of Summer, the girl from another world who had turned the dwarves' lives so completely upside down. *She* had arrived in Presadia through a magic mirror.

"Hello?" Antimony called into the silence after the curious disembodied voice had finished its silly rhyme.

There was no response – just the twinkling of shards beneath the rubble.

After Summer, her friend Jonah had arrived. It was Jonah who had seen how the dwarves were taking advantage of others to make their money. The two children had challenged the dwarfish high ruler Tin, who had been so moved and horrified that he had declared, there and then, that the dwarves must change their ways and do everything in their power to aid the people who had been hurt by their actions. He'd pledged to help the children find a way back to their own world; a promise that had led them high into the mountains to seek the wisdom of Khoree, an ancient and terrifying dragon.

One thing had led to another, and before Antimony could say "great beards below", Tin, his high ruler, had been flying off with the dragon and children on a grand quest to find the long-lost king, to see if he knew a way to get the children home. Antimony, Salt, and the others had waved goodbye in a state of befuddlement, wondering how so much could have happened in such a short space of time.

Being dwarves, they hadn't wasted time scratching their beards, but had decided to crack on with something productive. They had come straight to the castle from the dragon's lair, not wanting to waste a second in carrying out their high lord's command. They had wrongs to right and people to help, and any dwarf worth his pickaxe knew they needed to roll up their beards and get stuck in.

Well, metaphorically speaking, anyway. Antimony didn't actually have a beard yet. He was sure it would come soon. A growth spurt must surely be just around the corner. He was almost fifteen summers old already, yet only a few wispy whiskers clung hopefully to his spotty chin. Ma had assured him that late bloomers often boasted the best and longest beards in the end. Her own beard had been short and unimpressive until her thirtieth summer, when it had undergone a growth spurt so rampant that now, many years later, she was a member of the dwarfish high council by virtue of having the sixth-longest beard in Val-Chasar! Antimony dreamed of the day he would have a beard like that.

The daydreams didn't stop him feeling self-conscious about his naked chin, though. Thankfully, no one made a point of it. It was much like the way they accepted that he was a little taller than most dwarves. OK, *much* taller. In fact, he towered above his friends. Even so, Antimony was as valued as the next dwarf, particularly for his quick, mathematical brain, which High Lord Tin himself often relied upon. No one in Val-Chasar could balance a tricky ledger more quickly than Antimony, or work out the most efficient mechanics for a new invention. Dwarves prided themselves on ingenuity and being masters of design. In that, at least, Antimony was the gold among the bronze.

An unexpected movement in the rubble below made him jump. Awkwardly balanced as he was, he slipped and fell backwards.

2

RESCUE

Antimony laughed as Copper pulled funny expressions and made squeaking noises – a different sound for each of the plaited strands of his beard. Antimony loved this game, and it warmed Opal's heart to see them play together. He would pull on one of the plaits and squeal in delight at his pa's response. She chuckled too, more in reaction to her son's laughter than anything else.

Her son. Her treasure. The most precious gift ever given to her.

The giggling stopped as the game ended, and Antimony snuggled up on his father's lap. Despite being only two winters old, he was already much bigger than the other children his age. Opal's husband was humming a mining song, one of Antimony's favourites. Their son played with the beads in Copper's beard, counting them in time to the mining chant. Opal was filled with pride. Other children might have the first hairs of their beards coming through, but Antimony was unique among his friends in being able to count already. She would ask him how many tools were hanging on the wall, or how many mushrooms were in his bowl, and he always knew the right answer. He could even add and subtract, unheard of in a dwarf so young.

Opal was thankful for this unexpected skill, because sometimes she worried about her son. He didn't like the things other dwarves his age enjoyed. He couldn't pick up the stone toys and he wasn't interested in the wooden pickaxes.

Antimony was... different.

She pushed her worries to one side.

It didn't matter. He was who he was, and that was all that was important: Antimony, her gem and her world.

"Aha! You found me. How delightful. I hope you enjoyed my song."

"Hello? Yes. Yes, it's OK. We'll get you out." Scrabbling to regain his footing after the sudden appearance of the grimy face below him, Antimony's mind was already puzzling over how he was going to achieve that. Great beams were wedged between the ruined walls of the tower. A section of the castle battlements rested precariously on top of them, as well as a heap of rubble. It all looked ready to tumble down at any moment.

"Stay still and er... try not to move anything. We'll get you out in no time, but we don't want to cause a cave in. Salt! Salt! Come over here! I've found someone."

There was a vague outline in the shadowy hole, of a face that was observing him with interest. It was framed by the glittering shards, which somehow caught the light despite being deep in the gloom of the small space. It reminded Antimony of a geode: a rock that was dull and ordinary on the outside but, when broken open, looked like tiny caves whose walls were formed of thousands of sparkling crystals.

"The king's blessing upon you, friend. I wondered if anyone would hear me."

"I heard, and I'm here now, so don't worry. Is there anyone else with you?"

"No, no, just me," replied the man, his voice calm and cheery.

Antimony wondered again if the man had been driven crazy by what had happened. After all, he thought, if their roles had been reversed and *he* had been the one buried alive by a falling tower, he would have been a blithering mess. Yet this man wasn't displaying any of the distress the other survivors had shown. In fact, he didn't seem bothered in the slightest by his predicament.

Staying calm was a good thing, though, considered Antimony. A panicky person, struggling among the rubble, might easily cause the whole lot to come tumbling down.

"Sit tight. We'll get you out."

"I don't think I can do much else down here."

Salt came toward them, puffing and panting as he heaved and clambered his way over and around the various obstacles, finding it harder going than Antimony had done. Long arms and legs counted for something at least.

"Oh good, good, my dear boy. You've found another one? Well done! I thought we had already found everyone."

"There's a man down here, buried under the tower," Antimony told him.

"Oh dear, oh dear. A sorry situation to be in if ever there was one. He must be feeling quite down in the dumps, eh?" The boisterous dwarf chuckled at his own joke before Antimony's serious face silenced him. "Of course, of course. No laughing matter."

Salt reached the doorway and Antimony pointed out the small hole and the man in his glittering prison.

"That must be half the tower on top of him," muttered Salt. "It will take dozens of dwarves hours to move all that rubble. It's coming up to evening already…"

Antimony examined the heaped rubble, his mind working of its own accord.

Limestone masonry… that's around four hundred and fifty heavy weights

18

per cubic span… The beams are oak… They must be at least two hundred heavy weights at that size…

"Well," said Salt, drawing a heavy breath, "we can't just stand around here and do nothing. The sooner we start the sooner we will get him out of there. Stay with him, lad. I'll go and gather more help."

He set off in the direction of the dwarves' temporary camp in the remains of the castle courtyard.

"Hold tight!" Antimony called down to the man. "We're getting more help."

"Can't *you* help me?" the voice asked.

Antimony looked at the mountain of debris balanced precariously above the man. Once again, without prompting, his brain did what it always did: the mathematics. In reality, it was all just a case of balance and chain reactions.

Removing that large stone there would allow that beam to shift ten degrees or so to the left. That would free up space to…

A few carefully planned moves might achieve as much as an army of dwarves simply hefting it all piece by piece.

"Hello?" the voice from the hole called. "I don't mean to hurry you, but it's rather uncomfortable down here. But then again, as the young dwarf discovered, it's easier to see the light when you are surrounded by darkness."

"Yes," Antimony replied distractedly, "I'm just…"

Aha! That should work.

He thought through his plan once more. He would need to be careful. Moving the wrong thing – or even the right thing too far – could bring everything tumbling down, burying the poor man forever in his underground prison.

"Keep still," he instructed again before climbing onto the debris.

Carefully positioning each foot and hand onto the points he had calculated were safe – sections that shouldn't cause the precariously balanced rubble to shift or move – he climbed cautiously across. His first target was a smallish chunk of masonry. Stooping over it, he heaved. It was heavy, but he didn't need to lift it entirely. Easing it onto a splintered floorboard that was wedged at an angle, he slid it out of the way. Grunting, he pushed and shoved enough to extract the remains of a sturdy wooden chair, carefully placing it to one side. Now, if he could just lever that beam a few hand-breadths…

There was a crash as a dangerously balanced boulder on the other side of the tower dislodged. Sweat ran down Antimony's forehead as he tensed at the noise and the skittering of other debris falling into the gaps. However, this was exactly what he had calculated would happen. He took a moment to catch his breath.

"Mind before muscle," he reminded himself. They were words his pa had once said to him when he was small and struggling to do the things other dwarves found easy with their stocky, well-muscled arms. Antimony's arms had always been weedy and decidedly lacking in muscle. His father had always encouraged him to use his brain and near-perfect memory, and not to compare himself with the other dwarves. He missed his pa so much. He'd been only six when the mine caved in and his father never returned home. Antimony was thankful that his memory was especially good. It meant he could replay the conversations and times with his father almost as if he were still there.

Mind before muscle.

That little piece of wisdom had become the story of Antimony's life. When it became clear he wasn't built for mining – he was too tall and gangly to be of much use in the mines – his ma had arranged for him to work in the dusty library of Val-Chasar, checking entries in the big ledgers and keeping records in order. The librarian soon came to appreciate his quick mind, and he was given the job of drawing up plans for the many contraptions dreamed up by the inventive dwarves. His skills of logical reasoning hadn't gone unnoticed by the high council, who had recently sent him out with the trading caravans to assess whether they could be made more profitable.

He enjoyed numbers and he liked his work. But often he would look at other dwarves his age and wish he could be like them and have the physical strength they had. The fact that he didn't even have a beard only made it worse. Life would have been so much easier if he could just be like every other dwarf.

Mind before muscle.

A door, ripped from its frame but wedged upright, fell with a loud clatter, causing smaller stones and objects to tumble unexpectedly. That *hadn't* been in his plan. Antimony waited for the movement to settle and adjusted his calculations before continuing with the next move.

There was a rumble as his last move see-sawed a large beam that had blocked the survivor's hole. With a final shove, he slid the beam to one side, exposing the hole in the ground. The messy pile of wreckage looked barely disturbed, but it no longer trapped the man in the pit.

Antimony grinned down into the hole, pleased. The filthy survivor returned his smile, a knowing twinkle in his eyes, as if they were old friends. But Antimony was certain he had never seen the stranger before in his life. He never forgot a face; never forgot anything he had seen. Not that there was much of the man's face showing. A hood covered his head, and his clothes were shabby, streaked with dust and ash from the ruins. To his credit, he had a beard. It was unkempt, covering the lower half of his face in crazed tufts that suggested it had not been cut in a very long time.

Antimony stretched out a hand to help him out of the pit. The man grasped it with a strong grip, pulling himself up. Antimony's hand tingled. His tired muscles seemed suddenly stronger as he heaved the survivor up and out of the mess.

"Thank you, my friend. A thousand thank yous! The king's own blessing be upon you. You risked yourself to save me. That was a noble thing."

"It was nothing," said Antimony awkwardly. "I'm just glad we found you."

"Not as glad as I am!"

The man chuckled and stretched, rolling his shoulders and moving his head from side to side as he savoured his new-found freedom. Antimony watched for a moment before realizing he was staring.

"Erm… Good. Well, er… let's get you over to the… erm, main camp," he said hesitantly. "We have plenty of… erm… food and water. You must be hungry and thirsty."

"Your kindness will not be forgotten, my friend," the man replied in his sing-song tone. "But I wonder if I might beg one more kindness from you?"

"Erm… well… of course." Antimony was feeling increasingly self-conscious under the man's gaze. "Happy to… er… help."

Despite the tattered rags, filthy face, and crazed beard, the man had a commanding presence, controlling the situation as if *he* had been the rescuer rather than the one needing to be rescued. A sudden thought struck Antimony. Perhaps this man was the lord of this castle. He certainly had the regal assurance of a ruler, despite his humble appearance.

The man gestured at the hole he'd now vacated. "I wonder if you could gather up the mirror shards down there for me. They are more valuable than everything else in this castle combined!" He spread his arms wide and spun on the spot before stopping and fixing Antimony with a serious stare. "They have real magic, you know. Help me in this, Antimony, and I will be forever grateful."

For some reason, Antimony found he wanted to please this mysterious stranger, in spite of the growing suspicion that he was a lunatic. He responded, therefore, by dropping down into the small hole, which glittered with the scattered shards. Could they really be magic? Antimony would have dismissed the idea as the ramblings of a man a few wheels short of a mine cart if it hadn't been for meeting Summer and Jonah in equally peculiar circumstances. It was a magic mirror that had brought them to Presadia. Perhaps…

It was only as he reached the bottom and crouched in the small space that he realized something. The man had used his name.

"How did you know…?" Antimony looked up out of the hole, his voice trailing off mid-sentence.

The stranger was gone.

3

BEAUTY IN BROKENNESS

Zil poked her way through the ruins where her room had been. It was nothing more than a scorched pile of timbers and sooty stones now.

It had happened again, just as it had before. War. Stupid, stupid war! It had taken her parents and her old home. It had forced her out of her village. Then, just when she thought her luck had turned, just when she was rebuilding her life in the castle, it had all been destroyed again. For what? Probably ten paces of land on a greedy lord's border.

Everything she'd had and everything she knew had been taken from her. It always was.

Zil didn't know what the future had in store for her, but she wouldn't just roll over. She wouldn't let war beat her. She would make her own life. A new life. Far, far away from here.

She sighed.

Maybe one day.

She turned from the remains of the burned-down servants' hall and considered her options. The pesky dwarves were crawling all over the ruins, trying to look noble and kind. They were offering food and shelter to the survivors from the castle and surrounding villages, all of whom were now homeless.

How very kind of them, thought Zil scathingly. If it hadn't been for them the war between Lord Raven and Lord Brookford would probably never have happened. Everyone knew dwarves stirred up trouble so they could sell their wares. They were no better than common thieves in her eyes.

But Zil didn't have many other options. From the castle hill she could see that all the surrounding villages had been looted and burned. She didn't really know anyone else around these parts; only a few of the other serving girls and people from the castle. If the dwarves were offering food and a bed, well, maybe accepting kindness from thieves was better than an empty stomach and a night among the ruins.

Driven more by hunger than reason, she stomped her way across to the dwarves' wagons.

"Hello?" Antimony called again. The man must have gone to stretch his legs after his long imprisonment. Still, Antimony couldn't help but think that the whole meeting had been a little strange. He couldn't really put his finger on why, but the man was like no one he had ever met before. How had he known Antimony's name? Had he heard Salt use it?

He shrugged to himself and looked around at the broken pieces of mirrored glass that the man had said were so valuable. They didn't look valuable. Or magical either. They were just fragments of a broken mirror. Hundreds of them, spread around him like a torn-up carpet. He noticed then that some pieces had been deliberately wedged and balanced among the broken timbers and blocks of stone, presumably by the strange man. Out of boredom perhaps?

Or through some strange reasoning of his crazed mind? Antimony looked closer. The carefully positioned shards flashed, reflecting the light from the entrance hole. Rainbows of mesmerizing colour bathed the dusty space, creating beauty from the brokenness.

Antimony gasped in wonder. It really was like being inside a geode!

He saw now that the broken pieces had been artfully arranged. The miserable surroundings only made the mirror fragments shine more brightly. Maybe the man was a genius rather than crazy. Antimony wasn't sure he would be able to tell the difference.

Carefully, not wanting to cut his hands on the sharp edges, he started to gather up the pieces of glass and place them into his empty food bag. As he prised a piece from a section of ornately painted frame, he thought he caught the reflection of a crying baby in its glittering surface. Surprised, he turned around, but there was nobody there.

Another reflection flashed at the edge of his vision. His ma and... and his pa. Ma was holding a lantern aloft in a dark mine shaft, the light falling on a small baby in his father's arms. The image was gone before Antimony could take a proper look. Another flicker and there was a toddler, taller than the dwarves around him and without the wispy baby beard the others had on their chins. Then a tall, gangly child, surrounded by his friends as they marvelled at his mathematical workings-out.

Another memory flashed up of Antimony helping to change the fading glow-stones on the ceiling of a tunnel – a job the other dwarves needed ladders and teamwork to complete. Then, there he was, cross-legged at the dining table, his parents smiling lovingly. Next he was poring over books in the library, then struggling to help in the mines. Hundreds of memories came flooding in, as crystal clear as the day they had happened, yet too fleeting to fix his attention on.

Antimony blinked. He had a remarkable memory, everybody said so. Yet this was something different. Something magical.

He caught a glimpse of Khoree the dragon flying across Presadia. Below her mighty wings, in a basket made with Antimony's help, were the children, Summer and Jonah. Alongside them was Tin, the dwarfish high lord. Below them, the kingdom stretched vast and distant, and choked by the yellow fog that had become a normal part of life in Presadia. His friends vanished, and for the briefest of moments Antimony saw a dark place surrounded by a storm. Then it was gone, in a blaze of light that made him blink and left purple dots across his vision.

Then came another vision. Like a memory, yet Antimony knew this had never happened. He was walking among ruins far older than the castle he was in now. The ruins were overgrown and moss-covered, almost reclaimed by the forest that had grown up around them. As that image faded, another flickering shard showed the same ruins, only this time they were restored. No longer did roots and weeds grow up around the masonry; instead, whitewashed walls rose majestically over tidy gardens. There were golden turrets with jewelled domes and, at the heart of the castle, a fantastic, twisting tower spiralled up to an incredible height.

"Antimony?" Salt's voice broke the spell.

Antimony looked up, groggy and disorientated, as if awoken from a deep sleep.

"Antimony?" Salt said again, peering down into the glittering yet gloomy hole. "What under earth are you doing down there? Where's that poor fellow gone? Oh my, don't tell me he's been crushed! Of course not. We would have heard the screams. Did you manage to get him out all on your own? Remarkable, my dear boy! You never cease to amaze me."

Salt could merrily continue a whole conversation by himself. Antimony sat in silence, trying to make sense of the strange pictures in his head. The final image of the outlandish, captivating palace was ingrained in his memory as clearly as if he had been there that very afternoon.

"But what in Great Potash's beard possessed you to go down there yourself? It's filthy. Not to mention that it looks as though this could all tumble down any moment. Come along, lad. I've gathered the others. We should be good to head back to Val-Chasar and our nice hard beds. Where did your new friend go, anyway?"

"My new friend?" Antimony frowned, befuddled, as though he had been roused from a strange dream.

"Yes, the chap in that pretty pit of yours."

"I… I don't know."

"How rude!" Salt scoffed. "Typical, I tell you. No one thanks a hero. I've rescued a fair few people in my time, I can tell you. Well, never mind. Come along. It's time to head home if we want to be back by nightfall. On the way I'll tell you about the time I rescued a little girl from an angry centaur. Though in truth I think the centaur may actually have been in greater danger…"

"Coming," Antimony replied. "I'll catch up and meet you by the wagons."

"What? Oh, very well. Don't be long, and do be careful! I don't want to have to tell your mother you're buried under a castle. She terrifies me. I'll tell the others we are ready to go."

Salt disappeared from view and Antimony quickly gathered up every piece of the magic glass. He didn't see any more visions, but he didn't need to; the gloriously restored palace was vivid in his mind, more real than reality itself. Antimony longed to see it again. He cast hopeful glances into the final few broken shards as he gathered them up, but was met with nothing more than snatches of his own grubby reflection.

He remembered Summer and Jonah's story about arriving through a mirror from another world. Khoree the dragon had said the king once made magic mirrors people could travel through; mirrors that showed glimpses of truth, mystery, and even visions of the future. They had set out to find the king in the hope that he could help Jonah and Summer find their way home again, but no one really knew if the king was still alive.

Antimony stared at the shards, glittering in his bag. Could this be the same mirror? Maybe if he repaired it the two children would be able to use it to go home to their own world. He must do it, he decided. He must try to repair the mirror in the hope that it might help the children, if and when they returned to Val-Chasar.

4

THE MIRROR PUZZLE

Zil looked around the dingy, small cave the dwarves called home. It was like no home she had ever seen before. It was circular, with a bench around the edge. Opposite the front door was a large hearth and several smaller doors that led to other rooms. Zil hadn't looked through those yet. Over their heads, the walls curved up to form a dome with a glow-stone at the centre. Antimony had stretched a shade across it to dim the room for sleeping.

The dwarfish home had already been filled with human refugees when she arrived with the rest of her group from the castle. The survivors, including Zil, had been divided into groups at the wagons and led away to stay in various dwarves' homes. Zil's group had been told to go with the one they called Antimony. Now the little cave was practically bursting at the seams.

Antimony. He was the oddest dwarf Zil had ever seen. She had travelled on his wagon and then followed him through Val-Chasar to this strange little cave house. Even in such a short time she had learned that he was obsessed with numbers and complex connections. Half the time she had had no idea what he was talking about as he led them to his home. And she wasn't sure dwarves should be that tall. All the other dwarves treated him as one of their own. None of them appeared to question his dwarfishness, but, although he dressed like a dwarf, talked like a dwarf, and clearly thought of himself as a dwarf, Zil couldn't help wondering if there was more to his story than met the eye.

It had been night-time when they arrived in the famous canyon city. A thousand lights from windows in the cliff had made Val-Chasar look like a river of glimmering stars. Golden statues and jewelled carvings glittered and twinkled in the reflected light of the lamps and glow-stones. Such a sight should have filled her with awe, but for Zil its splendour was tainted by the knowledge that it had all been built on the suffering of others. Dwarves were greedy and manipulative, and she would not let herself be tempted to think otherwise simply because they had built such a beautiful city.

Despite her reservations about the dwarves, Zil had been relieved to reach Antimony's home. His mother, Opal, had greeted them like honoured guests and given them big bowls of mushrooms to eat. She had apologized profusely about the crowded conditions, hurriedly making up extra sleeping pads – little more than folded blankets – on the floor of the main living area, the bedrooms already being full of other refugees. It wasn't exactly luxurious, but Zil had warmed to Opal's hospitality in spite of her determination to disapprove of dwarves.

Now she lay back on her sleeping pad, listening to the gentle snores of the other humans and frowned to herself as she wondered about everything that had happened that day. Was this kindness of the dwarves genuine? She'd always been told they were meddling, selfish, spiteful creatures. For the moment, though, food and shelter were all she wanted. She would worry about everything else tomorrow.

✿

Closing the door, Antimony breathed a sigh of relief. Never had their small home housed so many people. He hadn't realized Ma had already filled all their spare rooms with many of the other homeless villagers who had been trickling into Val-Chasar. He felt a little guilty about the humans sleeping in the main living room. He had almost expected to have to share his small bedroom with one of the homeless humans, but was quietly thankful that Ma had kept that clear for him. His room was his sanctuary.

Antimony liked people. He liked them a lot. But they didn't always understand him and he didn't always understand them. Not many people shared his fascinations, and working out what other people were feeling was a tricky business. It was a relief to be alone, able to focus on his own thoughts without distractions. Despite the long, tiring day, he was itching to get out the mirror fragments and begin piecing them together.

"First things first," he muttered to himself as he opened the lantern cage beside the door. He reached inside to tickle Sparks, his pet magma-worm. She was a large worm – about the length of his hand and wider around her girth than most, with scales like stone shingles. Between these, her inner fire glowed through her translucent skin. The light was dull at the moment, only a faint orange glow outlining each scale, which meant she was probably asleep. Antimony would need more illumination for the challenge ahead.

"Hello, Sparks," he said, smiling at her. "You're looking sleepy tonight."

He scratched under her chin affectionately with his forefinger, feeling her heat on his fingertips. Sparks awoke and wriggled with pleasure, her glow brightening and filling the room with light. As she grew brighter, she also grew hot. Very hot! Antimony snatched his finger away and popped it in his mouth. It always hurt a little, but he was used to it and his fingertip had become tough from the years of looking after her. Most dwarves could boast a burn-hardened index finger from tickling magma-worms. Nothing was as effective or reliable deep in the caves, where torches could run out of oil and glow-stones did not shine brightly enough.

Antimony retrieved some mushrooms he had taken from the big bowls Ma had prepared on their arrival. He sprinkled them with a little coal dust from a saucer beside the lantern and fed them to Sparks. She gobbled them down instantly and he gave her a few more. She ate a lot these days. He had never heard of a fat magma-worm, but Sparks was certainly packing it away.

He closed the lantern and pushed his things back against the walls to make some space on the floor, then sat down in the middle of the room. His fingers fumbled with excitement as he opened his bag and gently tipped the glass fragments into a glittering, tinkling heap on the bare stone floor.

He paused, watching the pile for a few moments in case the magic mirror shards did anything special again. Nothing happened. He wasn't sure whether to be disappointed or not, but he set to, carefully spreading them out so he could see each individual piece. He had been thinking about them all the way home in the wagon, and this felt like finally scratching an itch after a long few hours of waiting.

It was a painstaking task, attempting to work out where the broken pieces fitted together. Antimony knew he should be sleeping, but his brain was far too alert. He told himself he would make a start – that was all; just work on it for a little bit.

His mind was racing, captivated with the challenge of piecing together the broken mirror and thinking over the meeting with the strange man and the curious visions. After climbing out of the pit, he had searched the ruins for the stranger, but he was nowhere to be found. It made the whole meeting even more puzzling, but

Antimony didn't pretend to understand people, let alone non-dwarves. Perhaps all humans were that odd.

Antimony started with the bigger pieces of mirror, of which there were quite a few. He picked up each one, examining it and memorizing the shape before trying to find its neighbour among the glittering collection. It was as if he sat at the centre of a stone-floor ocean. Mirrored islands surrounded him and cast rainbows over the walls and ceiling; islands that started small but gradually increased in size as, fragment by fragment, he matched one broken piece to another.

He lost all track of time. Lines, angles, and glittering shapes filled his mind, and the puzzle compelled him to keep going.

Piece by piece.

Bit by bit.

Broken shard by broken shard.

Visions from the ruins played over and over in his head as he worked, always coming back to the image of the palace. He would see it: tumbled-down, abandoned, forgotten – and then gloriously and splendidly complete.

As the hours passed, Sparks grew dozy and the light dimmed. When Antimony could barely see, he got up and stretched his stiff arms and legs. Apologetically, he woke the sleepy magma-worm again and looked down at his handiwork. He had assembled a number of largish islands now, but he couldn't fit them together. There was still a heap of smaller shards. They were proving tough.

Now he was standing up, however, he could see patterns within the chaos. His eyes darted over the puzzle. Something in his brain clicked.

"Of course," he muttered under his breath. "It's basic fractography." He had read that word in one of the dusty books in Val-Chasar's little-used library. Sometimes he felt as if the long-dead dwarves who had written those books were his friends.

Among them were historians and mathematicians, philosophers and politicians. His favourites were the mathematicians. Geniuses like Titanium Arithmabeard and Adamite the Counter were more inspiring to Antimony than any hero from the old stories.

"Titanium Arithmabeard's law of distributed force…"

In his head he recalled the pages of the book, bringing to mind the image he wanted with perfect clarity, a skill that never ceased to amaze the other dwarves. It wasn't unusual for Antimony; he had always been able to remember things perfectly, in as much detail as when he had first seen or heard it. It was why he was so good at mathematical puzzles.

"When a material is fractured from a single point of impact, the force of impact will spread out from the centre." Antimony recited the words to himself as if reading them directly from the page of the book, even though he hadn't seen it in years. "The force is distributed, reducing in intensity the further it is from the source."

He remembered a diagram from the book. It had resembled a spider's web, each segment growing larger as it moved out from the centre point.

Looking down at the mirror islands, he imagined them to be like parts of a spider's web. His brain reshuffled the parts.

Yes!

With renewed energy he dropped to his hands and knees and rearranged his glass islands. The biggest pieces he moved to the edges, the smaller and more fragmented shards toward the centre of the mirror.

His hands couldn't keep up with his brain. Yet despite his slowness in moving the sharp shards, the shape of the tall mirror quickly emerged. The smaller pieces at the centre took longer, but his hands were fumbling with excitement by the time he came to put the final few pieces in place.

And then… *No!*

Please, no.

It couldn't be.

His eyes scanned the floor in desperation. He grabbed his bag and searched around inside before tipping it upside down and shaking it hard.

It was no use. One piece – one single piece from the very centre of the broken mirror – was missing.

5

THE MISSING SHARD

Mmmmmmm.

Sparks dozed, unaware and unthinking. She was never really aware or thinking. She didn't know how long she had been dozing. She didn't really know anything. Except that it wasn't time yet.

She sensed something changing. It was only the vaguest of sensations, not really a thought. She didn't have those.

Sparks slumbered on a moment longer. He was back. She knew him; he was nice to her. He fed her. That was something she knew. *Hunger.* She was always hungry now. Had it always been like that?

Strange, that was almost a thought. She hadn't had one of those before.

She felt a pleasant sensation. He was tickling her under her chin and behind her ears.

Mmmmmmmmmmm, she thought again.

That feels good.

With a bitter sense of disappointment, Antimony slumped down in his sleeping place – a comfortable section of bare stone floor.

Dwarves didn't need all those unnecessary mattresses and sleeping pads that humans liked. It was unnatural to sleep without being connected to the solid stone beneath him. The comfortable rock didn't ease his body into sleep that night, though. All he felt was frustration.

He let out a deep sigh. All that hard work, all that time and energy, for nothing! The mirror was incomplete and Antimony couldn't fix it.

It was more than just the annoyance of not having finished an ordinary puzzle or challenge. The mirror puzzle had felt like Antimony's one chance to help Summer and Jonah in their quest to return to their own world. Now if they came back, all Antimony had to offer was a useless pile of glass.

He closed his heavy eyes, utterly exhausted.

The picture of the restored palace still fluttered before his closed eyelids, teasing him, and when he eventually dozed off, it was that same enchanting vision that filled his dreams.

He awoke suddenly, unsure what had woken him. For a moment he lay still, looking up at the rough stone ceiling. Sparks' glow was faint, but gave him just enough light to see by. Turning his head, he gazed across the room.

He jumped violently.

He scrambled backwards and pressed his back against the wall with a stifled yelp. Standing only a few short paces from him was a hooded stranger. No, wait, it was *the* hooded stranger. The man Antimony had rescued from the ruins. He was examining the pieced-together mirror shards, oblivious to Antimony's alarm.

"Who are you? What are you doing here?" Antimony's heart was pounding in his chest. How had the man got into his bedroom? Antimony was sure he hadn't been on the wagons with the other survivors.

The man seemed unconcerned by the strangeness of the situation, just as he had been in the ruins. In fact, he gave the impression that Antimony's bedroom was exactly where he was supposed to be at that moment. A mischievous grin lit his face. Ignoring Antimony's questions, he muttered a little rhyme:

> *"A pot filled with cracks leaks whatever's inside.*
> *If you think that I'm cracked, then my cracks I won't hide."*

He looked round at Antimony, as if surprised to find him there. "Oh! Good evening, Antimony. I must say, this is beautiful work." He stooped down to run his fingers over the cracks. "It must have taken great care and hard work to do this."

Antimony huddled in silence, lost for words. It felt awkward to simply repeat his questions. But then the whole situation was awkward. Who was this man? What did he want from Antimony? Perhaps he had come back for his mirror shards. But... how had he found their home and, more importantly, who had let him in?

"You are very gifted. Few people would have the patience and skill needed to restore something that looked so broken."

Antimony was still lost for words, but his eyes were drawn back to the incomplete mirror. Annoyance at the missing piece rose up in him as he looked down at his failed attempt.

"It doesn't *look* broken. It *is* broken."

"Oh, I've never let that stop me. To me it looks as if it's in the process of being mended. It's not finished yet, but it's no longer broken. Somewhere between broken and whole, perhaps."

Who was this madman? "But there's a piece missing. And it can never be properly mended anyway. I shouldn't have bothered trying. It was a waste of time."

The hooded intruder looked up at him and tilted his head, a curious expression on his face that Antimony couldn't read.

"Do you really think so?"

"Of course. I don't know why I tried. Even if it wasn't missing a fragment, it would still be broken. I thought piecing it all together would help, but… I don't know how to get rid of all the cracks."

"Perhaps getting rid of the cracks is not what you should be trying to do. *I* think it's beautiful, even with the cracks. They may not have been there before – should never have been there really – but now they *are* there, the cracks tell a story."

"What?" Antimony lifted his shoulders and let them fall again in a grumpy shrug. "A story of how it got broken and how I wasn't able to fix it?"

The stranger didn't reply. Instead, he lowered himself to sit cross-legged beside the mirror. Leaning forward, he ran his finger along one of the cracks. Where he touched, the mirror pieces beneath his fingers seemed to melt together. Antimony blinked in surprise. Where once there had been two pieces, there was now only one. Where the fracture had been, a thin line of silver glowed with an ethereal brilliance.

"When all the pieces are put back together," said the man, without looking up, "the cracks point to the one who cared enough to restore it. Knowledge of the brokenness makes us *more* aware of how wonderful it is than if it had remained unblemished."

He raised his head and smiled at Antimony. "When *I* look at this mirror, I see how lovingly and patiently you have worked to mend it. These cracks are no longer a sign of brokenness but a sign of restoration."

Once again, he dropped his gaze and continued his work, stroking each fractured edge to leave a path of glittering silver as the pieces joined together.

"Brokenness does not mean uselessness. It does not mean that the broken thing is worthless or that it is not treasured by someone. Why else do we mend things? We mend things because they are precious. We mend them because they are beautiful." He looked up at Antimony again. "Because they are of great value."

He paused before returning to his work. "Often it's only after something is broken that you realize how special it was to you and how important it is to restore it. Brokenness is not something to be afraid of, Antimony. Though cracks may be visible, they needn't be ugly. Cracks need not be a sign of shame and worthlessness; they can be a sign of love and wholeness restored."

Antimony stared, open-mouthed. He had seen master crafts-dwarves at work and marvelled at their almost magical skills when working on their masterpieces. This was more mesmerizing and awe-inspiring than any dwarfish handiwork. This didn't just feel magical; it was *really* magic.

Spellbound, he watched the man work the mirror beneath his fingers, moulding what should have been solid and unbreakable as easily as if he were a potter working with clay, or a blacksmith shaping molten metal. But there was no loud hammering here, or clanging of metal; this master craftsman's touch was gentle. It moved with the familiarity of someone who knew exactly what he was doing and with the tenderness of someone handling something incredibly precious.

"There will be times, Antimony, when you feel just as broken as these shards. When that happens, remember that you are not useless. You are deeply valuable. Anything that has been broken can be made whole again. Perhaps it won't look as it did before, and the cracks might still show, but so will the love that restored it."

Antimony's head brimmed with questions, but he didn't know how to start asking them. Something about being with the stranger made everything feel less pressing and important. He found himself content just watching the man mend the mirror.

It didn't take long. The stranger stood, breaking the spell. Reaching his hand into his rags he drew something out and offered it to Antimony. It was a single, small piece of glass.

The missing shard.

"You had it all along! But... why?"

"I was greatly impressed by your bravery and how well you used your head in the castle ruins. I wanted an excuse to come back and see you again, so I kept something back. I hope you can forgive me. You have worked hard on this mirror, and now it's yours. It's right that you should put the final piece in its place."

"It's mine? A-are you Lord Raven?" Who was this baffling man to give Antimony the mirror? He looked like nothing more than a ragged beggar, but acted like a generous lord bestowing a precious gift upon a faithful servant.

The stranger chuckled. "No, I am not Lord Raven. This mirror may have been in his castle, but it has a much longer history than that. A long time ago this mirror was in *my* possession. Indeed, I remember carving the frame and quarrying the single great shard of *majis-glatheras* to set within it."

"*Majis-glatheras*? That's king's glass. No one can cut that!" said Antimony.

"Oh really? No one told me that when I did it." The stranger winked and turned his gaze back to the almost-mended mirror, a look of pride on his face.

Antimony wasn't sure what to say or think. Perhaps the strange man was as crazed as the broken mirror, but Antimony couldn't deny the magical touch of a true master craftsman.

And he was still holding out the mirror shard to Antimony.

Hesitantly, Antimony took it. Stooping down, he pressed it into the small gap at the very centre of the mirror. It melted into the other pieces and the mirror was finally complete. Glittering lines where the cracks had once been glowed on the surface, as though a silver spider's web had been laid over the glass.

As the last piece settled into position the glittering web shone brighter. Rays of dazzling light pulsed out from the cracks.

Antimony scrambled back, shading his eyes. Even after he had closed them the light was bright enough to illuminate the red of his eyelids.

Then, as suddenly as it had burst forth, the light was gone.

Antimony blinked in the near darkness. Despite Sparks' glow, the light burst had left Antimony momentarily blind.

"What just happened?" he exclaimed as the bright after-images faded from his vision. "I can barely see a thing!"

The stranger didn't respond. It took a minute or so for Antimony's vision to clear enough for him to see that the stranger was gone without a trace. The room was empty apart from Antimony, Sparks' lantern, his few possessions, and the cobwebbed mirror.

Or, at least, there was something on the floor where the mirror had been. It was the same shape; the glittering lines where the cracks had been remained, but the reflective surface was gone. It had been replaced by a neat arch-shaped carpet of creeping vine. Around it, the smooth stone floor was exactly as it had been.

Antimony gawked. What was going on? Where had the man gone? And why, by Great Potash's beard, did Antimony now have a mirror-sized patch of greenery in his bedroom?

He rushed to the bedroom door and fumbled it open. The hallway was dark, and one of the homeless villagers was asleep on the floor. Light spilled out from the main room of the house. Antimony raced down the corridor to catch up with the man. He burst into the main room, scanning the space wildly as he searched for the stranger.

Antimony's mother jumped at his abrupt entrance.

"Fires below, Antimony!" she scolded. "You gave me a fright. What are you doing up so early? And why are you running about like a mad dwarf?"

"Where did he go – that man?"

"What man? There's no one here but us. Look, you've woken

them up now. Shame on you! But since you're up, I would appreciate a bit of help. Goodness knows I'm busy enough with all these extra council meetings lately, without cooking breakfast for sixteen people."

"But he must have come through here."

"What is up with you at the moment, Antimony?" Opal shook her head at his inexplicable behaviour. "And why are you chasing one of our guests, anyway? You're supposed to be making them feel welcome. This isn't like you. Now come and help me make breakfast."

Antimony's head hurt. What was going on? Where was the man?

Maybe it was he who was going crazy. Maybe it had all just been a strange dream.

"I... I can't. I have to..." He didn't finish the sentence, but turned and ran back to his bedroom.

6

THE FORGOTTEN PALACE

Opal stood for a moment, gazing after her son. Antimony had been behaving strangely of late. Perhaps he was having another of his unpredictable mood swings. It was as if he were somewhere between childhood and adulthood. He certainly wasn't a boy any more, but he wasn't grown up yet either.

He was more than grown up with regard to his height. There was no denying he towered above her. Antimony's... differences had become increasingly noticeable the older he grew. She knew the other dwarves wondered about him when she wasn't around, even though they had accepted and taken him in without question or complaint.

Antimony still seemed unaware of how different he was from the other dwarves. Opal felt a pang of guilt whenever she thought about that. She knew she should sit down and talk to him about it all, but she didn't know what to say or where to start. Every child thinks their parents have all the answers, but Opal was quickly learning that she didn't. All she knew was that she loved him more than anything and wanted everything to be right for him.

Antimony's erratic behaviour baffled Opal. What was she meant to do? If only his father – might he rest in peace – had still been around. Perhaps she should go after Antimony and have a mother and son heart-to-heart with him.

She looked down at her floury hands and the half-finished flatcakes. Her many guests, the human refugees – the king bless them – were getting up, and she still had to get the bread in the oven and shell the bowl of cave crabs she was planning to serve for breakfast.

Opal sighed, returning to kneading the flatbread and thinking about her son. Antimony would have to wait for the time being. She would talk to him later that day. Or maybe tomorrow.

Antimony closed the bedroom door. He knew it hadn't been a dream. The strange patch of greenery was still there. There was still no sign of the man.

Hesitantly, as if afraid the green archway would do something unexpected, Antimony inched his way across the room.

He reached down and plucked a leaf from the vine.

It was damp, small dewdrops clinging to it like miniature gems. His courage growing, he ran a hand across the plants, feeling the vines and leaves tickling his fingers. Rather than hanging down, the vines formed a horizontal curtain, beyond which was darkness.

He knelt down and gingerly pushed his arm into the greenery, his fingers passing through the glowing cracks. They felt like spider's webs breaking around his fingers, though the cracks remained exactly where they had been. Instead of a stone floor, there was only empty space. He reached a bit further, but an unexpected force on the other side of the fronds pulled his arm in a different direction. Not further into the floor, but toward the bottom edge of the arch. It was the weirdest feeling Antimony had ever experienced. Quickly he withdrew his arm. He had never read about *that* in Adamite the

Counter's *Observations on the Physics of Natural Forces*. Gravity was a force that pulled things downwards so they didn't float off. It didn't pull you sideways!

Carefully, he felt around the edge of the strange, green carpet. It was as if the cold stone of the floor itself were a frame around the vine-fringed void.

He slid his fingers into the arch-shaped hole, feeling under the edge. It seemed as though he could feel the underside of the stone floor – only a stone floor that was paper thin.

His mind raced back through every book he had ever read in the Val-Chasar library, which was a great many. He couldn't remember reading anything that explained this.

Hardly breathing, in case he broke the spell, Antimony slipped his whole hand under the edge. It was a weird sensation, watching his own hand vanish behind the stone floor.

He sat back on his knees while he thought, and an idea came to him. Running his hand across the top edge of the hole in the floor, there it was: a small lip, the same thickness as the mirror shards had been.

He managed to get his fingertips beneath the rim. Biting his lip in concentration, he strengthened his grip, slipped his whole hand beneath it and lifted. The vines swayed but remained unaffected by the gravity in his bedroom. Slowly – because it was heavy – he heaved the mirror upright.

Or what had once been a mirror. It was something else now. A window? A doorway? Antimony didn't really know. From behind, it felt to his hands like the mended mirror, and it weighed as much as a large mirror, but that didn't match what he saw with his eyes.

He leaned it up against the wall and stepped back to take a better look. The vines now hung downwards with gravity, not sideways as they had on the floor. He had never seen anything like this. Was this what Summer and Jonah had meant when they spoke of stepping through a mirror into another world? Was this some kind of magic portal? Was Summer and Jonah's own world on the other side of this arched opening? Had Antimony been successful in finding the children a way home?

His heart was pounding in his chest as he stared at the portal. It looked for all the world like an archway with thick vines and greenery hanging down on the other side. Behind them was darkness.

He reached out and parted the curtain of vines. The glow from his lantern illuminated a soft semicircle of grass beyond. He could just about make out the dark silhouetted canopy of a forest against a lightening sky. Dawn was breaking.

He turned back from the door and rushed over to Sparks' large lantern. His fingers fumbled with excitement as he opened the door and gave her a quick tickle. She wriggled, her light and heat bursting forth to flood the room with bright light. Closing the door again, he lifted the lantern from its hook and carried it toward the doorway. It was large and awkward, not really meant for carrying, but as he pulled the curtain aside again it illuminated the world beyond.

He took a deep breath and stepped through the portal.

The cracks brushed across Antimony's face and arms like the soft touch of silk on his skin. Beneath his feet, hard stone became soft grass. A light, cool breeze kissed his cheeks, a stark contrast to the still warmth from his cave bedroom, behind.

Stepping through gave him a better view of the world beyond. He was standing in a small glade of thick grass. Three sides of the glade were walled by massive trees with twisted limbs so large that their spreading branches almost enclosed the space entirely. Behind him was a cliff face covered in shrubbery and creeping vines. No, not a cliff – a quarry, thought Antimony as he cast his experienced eye over the stone. The cliff wasn't natural. Though time and weather had softened the edges of the cut stone, they were far too regular to be natural. A long time ago someone had used this place to quarry large chunks of stone.

Behind him he could see through the portal into his room. Around the doorway were the many facets and faces of a large deposit of *majis-glatheras*, so that the portal looked like a cave opening in the stone.

A bird hooted and Antimony heard the rustle of leaves. He turned to the forest again. The strange half-light – not quite day, not quite night – made the forest feel as though it was suspended in time. It gave Antimony the feeling he was between times, between worlds, between dream and reality. He could have been the only person in the world at that precise moment.

It felt... good. Peaceful. Exciting, even. Just moments earlier he had been anxious. Now it was as if his own thoughts were suspended in this place of in-betweenness. He felt... what? Expectancy? Anticipation? Rightness?

He stepped away from the portal and looked around him, increasingly aware of the noises and movements of the forest. After a brief hesitation, he made his way toward the forest. He didn't know where he was going, but that didn't matter. Antimony never really knew where he was going anyway, and he found himself somehow enjoying the magic of this unexpected place.

Was this Summer and Jonah's world; the place they had left behind when they came through the mirror? Antimony wasn't sure. It looked very much like his own country. There were other clues too. Despite the freshness of the air and the peace of the woods, there were traces of black mottling on many of the plants, the same disease that had spread over most of the plants and trees in Presadia. And although it was dark beneath the trees, Antimony could just make out tendrils of yellowy haze, another symptom of Presadia's troubles, weaving between the trunks of the trees to his left.

Antimony had spent some time with the children from the other world. Summer and Jonah had never encountered the black sickness or yellow mists before they came to Presadia. It had sounded to Antimony as if their world had its own problems, but the black trees and the mist were definitely Presadian problems. It seemed the mirror had taken him somewhere inside his own world.

A stream gurgled nearby. He headed toward the sound and found the water trickling its way through a small ditch filled with mossy stones and miniature waterfalls. Climbing down the bank, he stooped to dip his hands into the cool, clear water. It was rapidly growing lighter and the forest was waking with the dawn. The time between times was disappearing and a new day was starting, with chirps and rustles, distant animals calling to one another, creaky branches, sighing wind: a symphony of nature.

A flash of deep ruby and golden brilliance beneath the rippling water caught Antimony's attention. He jumped as he realized he was being watched by a reptilian eye. It stared up at him, unblinking and unnerving. He froze. He must have disturbed a creature from its slumber on the stream bed.

Ruby scales sparkled beneath the ripples around the eye. Antimony didn't dare move. After a long pause, he frowned. He could see only one eye; nothing else of the creature. He stooped down, reaching slowly through the water toward the creature. It didn't move. Ever so carefully, he touched the unblinking eye. It was cold and unmoving; just the weathered remains of a jewelled statue.

Reaching in with his other hand, he lifted a small but heavy slab of stone off the stream bed and out of the water, letting it fall onto the bank. Gemstones had been arranged in a fabulous and convincing mosaic to look like dragon scales. The gleaming eye was a large golden stone with a long black line down its middle. It looked just like a dragon's eye. Antimony knew because he had seen the real thing only days before on his visit to see Khoree the dragon, with High Lord Tin and the two children.

"This must be worth a pretty penny," Antimony said to himself, his voice breaking the stillness of the empty wood. But why was it here? And where was "here", for that matter?

Now he was paying more attention, he noticed other rocks and mossy lumps that were too regular to be natural boulders. He caught glimpses of similar carvings, hidden beneath nature's slow but unstoppable crawl. Part of a carved arm there, beneath the frond; a jewelled, bearded face covered in lichen, by that tree root; and a low, crumbled wall behind him, tree roots gripping it in wooden fingers.

He climbed away from the stream's edge and followed the trail of mysterious discoveries. The fragments of statues and carvings became bigger the further he went into the forest, and he could see large boulder-like chunks of masonry.

The trees gave way suddenly into a huge clearing filled with rubble, bits of weathered building, and a tall, even-sided hill. It looked to be perfectly round and had a flat top on which were the remains of a once-magnificent building. A familiar building.

Antimony stared up at it, his eyes wide.

He had seen it in his vision. He had seen it as it was now, and as it had once been; how it longed to be again.

The forgotten palace.

7

THE HIGH COUNCIL

Val-Chasar was like nothing Zil had ever seen. Every corner revealed a new marvel of dwarfish ingenuity or lavishness.

Her favourite part had been the main chasm, where the subterranean canyon city connected with the fresh air. It was the most awe-inspiring sight she had ever seen. In the daylight, it was even grander than she had thought the previous night.

The city was a complex example of dwarfish skill and imagination. Thousands of dwarves called it home, and it housed everything you might expect a city to contain: shops, storehouses, blacksmith caves, and taverns fronted onto roads and paths that zigzagged steeply up the cliffs. They were linked together across the gorge by hundreds of bridges: some rope bridges, swinging scarily; others elegant arches of carved stone, wide enough for two carts to pass side by side.

Factories, workshops, and businesses of all kinds had been built between the supports of the bridges and hung down like the dwarf ponies' shaggy coats. The windows and doors of houses pockmarked the cliffs and, deeper down, the gaping mouths of the mines swallowed metal tracks with their heavily laden wagons.

Despite the bustle, noise, and sheer volume of buildings crammed into the chasm, it was neither ugly nor cluttered. Quite the opposite, in fact. The dwarves took pride in the beauty of their city. Great murals and statues drew the eye. Roof gardens, plazas ,and fountains created quiet spaces for them to rest and relax in the warm twilight. Deep down, at the very bottom of the chasm, a small river wound around strange rock formations and dwarf-made lakes filled with fish and lake snakes.

It made Zil realize how small her world had been before. She had never seen so many people in one place. They were mostly dwarves, but she saw other humans too amid the hustle and bustle.

They looked like her: homeless and bewildered; unsure where to go or what to do. Their homes, their lives, had been destroyed by war or trouble and they didn't know what to do next. They looked sad and hopeless.

She didn't want to be like that. She didn't want to let what had happened define her or make her lose hope. But then she didn't really know what she did want. There didn't seem to be much to put her hope in.

Her stomach had led her back to Antimony's. She had been told there would be a midday meal for her if she wanted it. Exploring the city with its delicious smells rising up from the bakeries and street vendors had given her quite an appetite.

As she entered the cave-house, she was met by chaos. The room was stuffed full. Furniture had been pushed back and stacked up against one wall, and the human guests were squeezed into every gap they could find, most jammed onto the bench that ran around the wall. They were chewing on the strange dwarfish breadcakes and watching in fascination, clearly wondering whether they should be there at all. None of them looked as if they knew what was going on.

For some unknown reason, six thrones had been arranged in a circle. On each throne sat a dwarf with a tremendously long and full beard, all in the process of being groomed rapidly by other dwarves, as if each were racing the others to finish the grooming. It was, thought Zil, the most bizarre sight she had ever seen.

She spotted Opal and Antimony. Opal was sitting on a simple stool between two of the grand thrones and Antimony was frantically combing her beard while she hastily attached a number of hideously extravagant gold medallions into the freshly brushed hair.

"Oh... Zil, isn't it?" Opal called, seeing her standing in the doorway. "Lunch plans have changed a little, I'm afraid. Something's come up." She gestured to the chaos around her with a shrug, as if this were self-explanatory. "I'm hoping it won't last long, but apparently...". She glared at a stern-looking dwarf holding a huge, ancient book. "...We have to do everything by the book, which means full grooming and formal beards. I've put out a basket of flatcakes on the counter. Help yourself."

Zil stood in the doorway a moment longer, wondering if it would be better to leave. She didn't want to be in the way of this strange affair. Her stomach and curiosity made the decision for her, however, so she squeezed her way toward the basket before settling herself on the bench to watch the proceedings.

"Order! Order!" the chief groomer called.

He was a miserable-looking dwarf, carrying a humongous leather-bound copy of *Statutes and Principles*. Its rules instructed, in minute detail, how matters relating to the high council and high ruler were to be carried out. It was his responsibility to ensure that any meeting of the dwarfish high council was carried out in accordance with tradition and custom. This dwarf, Antimony had heard from his mother, was a stickler for the rules. Despite the uncommon circumstances and location, he had still delayed the meeting by more than an hour, insisting that the council members groom and don their official beard ornaments.

Antimony had heard about some of the strange rules from his ma, who had joined the high council five years earlier, when her beard had overtaken that of Lapis Longbeard at the annual measuring festival. The rules in the big book dictated precisely how beard length was to be assessed and strictly forbade any unnatural colouring. They required each council member to bring his or her own chair for a formal meeting, along with a thousand other strange rules.

The rule relating to chairs did not usually cause too many issues, since meetings were ordinarily held in the spacious council chamber at the high ruler's palace. Today was a different matter entirely, however, as the emergency meeting was being held in Antimony's living room. The other six council members had all turned up with their own chairs. That might not have been so bad if each member hadn't wanted to outdo the others, but the ridiculous thrones they had brought barely fitted into a circle in the usually spacious living room.

Ma wouldn't have dreamed of turning out the human refugees, so the living space that was usually just for Antimony and his mother was beyond overflowing. It was accommodating seven council members, seven helpers including Antimony, the chief groomer, six thrones, all their normal furniture, and a dozen or so human guests.

The noise was almost overwhelming. The chief groomer turned purple in the face as he tried to bring the chaos under some semblance of control.

"I said order! OOORRRRDDEEEERRRR!"

The hubbub finally quietened and the council members turned their attention toward the circle.

"This is highly unusual," Granite Greybeard, one of the council members, complained. "Council meetings should be a private affair. Holding this in someone's house before a crowd of gawking humans is highly inappropriate."

"Granite, I am surprised at you!" Opal scolded in a tone Antimony had heard many times growing up. "What would you have me do? Turn my guests out onto the street? Nonsense! Only last week High Lord Tin swore that we would do everything in our power to help these poor people. They have lost their homes because of us, remember."

Granite, old and grumpy, still looked unsatisfied. "I never suggested that, Opal. I merely think it would be more proper for the meeting to take place in the council chamber. What's this all about, anyway? It's most inconvenient to keep receiving formal summonses every few hours. All we seem to do is meet these days. Extraordinary meetings are becoming more ordinary than breakfast!"

"There has been a lot to discuss, particularly in High Lord Tin's absence," another of the council members, Andersite Thunderaxe, reminded him.

Ma nodded. "Quite so, and as for why we are meeting here, well, if you'll let me explain, Granite, you will soon understand my reasons."

"Oh, very well, very well. Can we please get on with it?"

"I intend to," said Opal.

Antimony found it interesting to watch his mother with the other council members. He knew about her work on the dwarfish high council – he'd even seen her with other council members performing some of her duties – but meetings like this were normally held behind closed doors. He felt proud at the dignity and authority with which she took charge.

"I have gathered you all here to discuss something most peculiar. You will all remember the children, Summer and Jonah, who arrived last week."

The council members nodded. How could they forget? The strange children from another world had stumbled into their lives, turned everything on its head, and then left on a quest to find the king, in the company of their high lord and a fire-breathing dragon. It was hardly an everyday occurrence.

"Summer told us they passed into Presadia through a magic mirror in Lord Raven's castle. Jonah informed us that the mirror shattered shortly after he arrived. Furthermore, dwarves who were at the castle reported that the tower housing the mirror was completely destroyed during the siege."

The council members were listening with a variety of expressions. Granite and a couple of others looked impatient or bored, clearly waiting for Opal to get to the point. Most looked respectful and inquisitive, intrigued as to why Opal was bringing up the subject of the magic mirror.

"The mirror clearly had magical properties. The dragon Khoree believed it to be one of the few, if not only, remaining mirrors created by the king himself before he was sent into exile. The legends say that he used these mirrors to watch over his kingdom and to travel around Presadia using magic. Like the mirrors, these magical powers have been lost to us."

"Enough of the history lesson, Opal. Get to the point," Granite grumbled.

She shot him an annoyed look and continued. "Yesterday, when returning from Khoree's lair, my son Antimony, in the company of a larger group of dwarves led by Salt, decided to go to Lord Raven's castle. Knowing the part they had played in causing the siege that destroyed it, they wanted to help in searching for survivors and bringing back those in need of food and shelter. Some of those people you see in this very room." She gestured toward the humans who were looking on.

Antimony glanced around, his gaze coming to rest on Zil. She was frowning, obviously listening closely to Opal's words.

"That was a good thing to do," one of the council members said, nodding at Antimony. The ancient dwarf was hairless apart from a thin silver beard, which was decorated with blue beads like a waterfall. "What we have done to the humans is shameful. We must continue to do all we can to help fix the problems we caused. To be reconciled with the humans, we must continue to act. Dwarves have always claimed to be faithful to the king, but our actions have proven otherwise. We have committed crimes against the king's law. We forgot the king's justice; and we must make amends."

The council members nodded sagely. Antimony wondered why the old dwarf was repeating something they already knew. Then it struck him. The old dwarf was probably speaking for the benefit of the homeless humans. They must have been finding it hard to trust the dwarves who had ruined their lives.

High Lord Tin had issued a decree. It had been read aloud on every street corner, and every dwarf in the city had heard it. Antimony himself had dug out an old copy of *The King's Law*, a thick book that explained the rules and commands for looking after the vulnerable. High Lord Tin had used this to explain how the dwarves were meant to be behaving, before listing the many things they were doing that went directly against that law. Tin had been brutally honest, including himself in the blame, and challenging each and every dwarf to stop and examine what they had become.

The letter had sent shockwaves through Val-Chasar and beyond. The dwarves had never really paused to question their way of life or to consider the impact it had on others. It was just how things were. Most dwarves never left Val-Chasar and had never seen for themselves what their lavish lifestyle and vast wealth was founded upon. It had really hit home when the first human refugees had been brought to the city. Seeing the ragged clothes and haunted expressions on their faces, the dwarves had finally understood the suffering their lifestyle had caused.

"Antimony," said Ma, jolting Antimony back from his thoughts, "was searching the ruins for survivors, when he came upon a man buried beneath one of the towers. It was the tower that had contained the magic mirror."

She paused, as if allowing the other council members to consider where the story was heading. Then she recounted the rescue and Antimony's discovery of the mirror shards. She described his vision of the broken palace restored. She spoke of how he had fixed the mirror. Finally, she shared how the mirror had opened up a portal, and how Antimony had gone through and found the abandoned ruins of the forgotten palace.

Antimony hadn't told her about the man appearing in his bedroom the night before. That encounter still felt slightly unreal to him. He felt silly talking about a person he believed was there but for whom no one else could find any evidence. They would probably have thought he was making up that bit.

When Ma reached the end of the story there was a long pause. Antimony felt everyone's eyes upon him. He blushed under their scrutiny.

Finally Andersite Thunderaxe spoke. "An unusual story, Opal. But more unusual than children from another world tumbling into our midst? I am quicker to believe after the events of the last week, but I would like to see for myself this mirror portal of which you speak."

"And speak to the man found with the shards," added Granite Greybeard. The other council members nodded in agreement to both requests.

"Of course you shall see the portal. That is the reason I called the meeting here in my home. The portal is in Antimony's bedroom, over there. As for the man, I'm afraid that won't be possible. He left shortly after his rescue and has not been seen again."

Antimony blushed again. That last bit wasn't exactly true, after all.

"Erm... actually..." he said hesitantly, embarrassed at the surprised look he received from the chief groomer, who had been frantically scribbling down the discussion in his big book until Antimony's unauthorized voice had spoken up.

He was about to tell him off but Opal spoke first. "Yes, Antimony?"

The chief groomer closed his mouth irritably. Now that Antimony had been asked a question by a council member he was allowed to speak.

"The... er... man."

"Yes?" This came from grumpy Granite.

"I did see him again. This morning. In my room. He had the final piece of the mirror. He... did something to make it whole again."

"Well, where is he now? This fellow clearly knows plenty about the mirror. We should question him."

"I don't know where he went. He fixed the mirror. It started glowing, and then when it stopped... well... he was gone."

"Gone where?"

"I don't know. Just gone. I thought he was in the house, but he wasn't."

"So who is he?" insisted another member of the council.

"I don't know," Antimony admitted.

"This boy doesn't know much at all!" grumbled Granite.

"Maybe the man passed through the mirror into the forest. We might find him there," one of the council suggested.

"Perhaps," Opal agreed. "We know little about this portal and the magic that makes it work. Antimony passed through unharmed, however, and found the very palace ruins he had seen in the vision."

Antimony plucked up the courage to speak again.

"I think the mirror is taking us there for a reason. I think we're supposed to rebuild the palace."

All eyes turned on him once again, including the hostile eyes of the chief groomer, who was pursing his lips, trying to decide whether Antimony's interruption was out of order and should be struck from the record.

The council members seemed less worried about protocol, however. Their expressions ranged from thoughtful and intrigued to sceptical and uncertain.

His mother broke the tension.

"I think before we discuss anything more or make any decisions about what to do regarding the mirror, we should all go to Antimony's room and see it for ourselves."

8

THE PORTAL

Zil had watched the council meeting with fascination. Who would have thought she'd be present at a meeting of the dwarves' high council? They were strange creatures. She had heard all sorts of stories about them. It had been common in her village for mothers to tell naughty children that if they were bad, a dwarf would come and snatch them away. Dwarves had stirred up the wars that had caused the destruction of her home. She had heard tell of how they had taken advantage of the most vulnerable by using the poor like slaves. Yet being here, well, the dwarves weren't what she had expected.

Opal and Antimony certainly weren't. Antimony was by no means a typical dwarf. They had been nothing but kind and generous in opening up their home and feeding the humans. The council members had seemed normal too. Even the grouchy Granite was no grumpier than many humans. They had expressed regret about their past behaviour and a desire to change; a desire they were clearly trying to live out.

She had mistrusted dwarves; hated them even. She had blamed them for many of the bad things that had happened to her. But being here in their city, in Opal and Antimony's home, well, it was making her think again. These dwarves weren't the evil, scary creatures she had been told about as a child. They had made some serious mistakes – they had acknowledged that themselves – and they certainly still had their quirks and issues. But in that respect, they were no different from humans.

Her belief that these people were not like her – were her enemies even – had made her look for the worst in them. She had expected them to be bad. But in truth they were not that different from her. She frowned at this thought, but was drawn back from her reflections by the seven council members getting to their feet and making their way through the crowded room toward Antimony's bedroom and the strange mystical portal they had been discussing.

Trying to move unnoticed in the crowded house, Zil followed. She wanted to know more about this magic mirror.

"I've never seen anything like it."

"Great chasm crabs! That's a mind-bender."

If the living space had been crowded, Antimony's bedroom was packed tighter than a barrel full of magma-worms by the time the seven council members, chief groomer, and Antimony had squeezed in to look at the mirror. The stuffy heat had awakened Sparks, who brightly illuminated the small room. They stared at the magical doorway and the quiet forest beyond.

"And you say Antimony went through?" one of the council members asked Opal.

Antimony and Ma nodded.

"Is this the world Summer and Jonah came from?"

"Perhaps we should send word that we've found them a way home."

"But we don't know where they are," Granite pointed out.

"They went to the Silverwood to enlist the help of the elves."

"Yes, but they rode there on a dragon. It would take more than a week for us to get there on foot, by which time they would be long gone. Not to mention that everyone knows the great forest has become far too dangerous to travel through."

"When I went through," Antimony chirped up bravely, "I saw signs of the tree sickness and the yellow fog."

The council members looked grim. They all knew about the sickness and unnatural fog that plagued the kingdom of Presadia.

"Presadia then, I think," Ma concluded. "Summer and Jonah didn't know about the sick trees and the yellow fog before they came here."

"But where in Presadia?" said Andersite Thunderaxe.

"We have no way of knowing without first scouting it out," said Opal. "Antimony's description of the palace he saw in his vision matches the legends of the long-lost king's palace, but we don't know exactly where it once stood any more. It was destroyed hundreds and hundreds of years ago."

"I can confirm that the few records we have from that time don't tell us specifically." The chief groomer looked smug at being able to use his knowledge of the dwarfish archives. "We have lost many of the books. The ones that mention the king's palace assume that the location is common knowledge. At the time no one felt the need to describe it in detail."

"There must be maps, though," said Granite.

"We only have fragments. Much of that section of the library was damaged in the great furnace fire during High Lady Nepheline's rule. We know it to be somewhere near the middle of Presadia, but that's all the information we have."

"The elves would know," said Opal. "They're immortal. Many of them would have actually been there at the time."

"But I just said, it would take a week or more to reach the elves, even if we made it through whatever dangers are lurking in the great forest. Who's to say the portal will stay open that long?"

There was a long pause as the council members looked over at the mirror portal and the wood beyond.

"So what do we do? Ignore it until the children return?" Opal asked.

"Go through," Antimony said when no one else spoke. "We need to restore the palace and make it like I saw in the vision."

"Nonsense!" scoffed Granite. "How do we know it's safe? What evidence is there that we'll be able to get back? Any dwarf who goes through could end up trapped in Great-Potash-knows-where! Not to mention that we no longer have a king. Why would we need a palace?"

"Khoree believed the king was still alive," insisted Antimony, surprised at his own boldness. "I was there when she told High Lord Tin, and…"

"I have little trust for that rude and irritable dragon," Granite interrupted, frowning at Antimony's outburst.

"What would you propose instead, Granite?" one of the other council members asked.

"I don't think it's safe; we don't know what's on the other side. If Antimony's right, it's simply an empty forest and abandoned ruins. I see no reason why we should risk our lives when there is so much work to do here, what with High Lord Tin's decree and all."

"There *is* still much to be done here," Opal acknowledged.

"But we *must* go through. The visions I saw…" Antimony protested.

"Antimony, my gem," Ma said kindly. "I believe what you saw, but these visions aren't necessarily saying we have to restore the palace. We don't know *what* they mean, or what kind of magic caused them. Perhaps the magic was simply showing you what it was like a long time ago."

"No!" Antimony didn't know how to describe the certainty he felt deep down in his belly. Their reluctance only made him feel more certain. "I can't say how, but I know we're meant to restore it. Why else would the visions have come to me? Why would this doorway open here?"

"Child," one of the other council members said, addressing him patiently but firmly, "repairing a palace would require many skilled dwarves and many more labourers. You must understand that we cannot undertake such a huge mission based on a feeling and a vague vision. For all we know, these 'visions' may have just been your imagination running wild."

Antimony's face grew hot. They didn't get it. It wasn't a daydream or his imagination. The visions had been real. The conversation with the strange man had only confirmed the growing conviction within him that he was destined to restore the palace.

"I agree," Andersite Thunderaxe said. "There are too many unanswered questions. Is the mirror working at random or does someone control it? What if it's in the power of someone who wishes us harm?"

"I cannot support the notion of sending dwarves through without receiving the answers to some of these questions," said Granite.

There were murmurs of agreement.

"So we do nothing?" Opal asked the group.

"We wait and see if anything happens, and we search the records for any references to magic mirrors," Granite corrected.

"I agree." The ancient council member with the beard that looked like flowing water nodded his approval.

The other council members nodded and grunted in agreement.

"It seems there is a majority of opinion," Opal said, her forehead creased.

"We can't just do nothing!" Antimony exclaimed in frustration.

Why didn't they get it? He felt more sure about this than about *anything* else in his life.

"Antimony," said his mother, "you are here because you discovered this magic doorway, but you are not a council member. The decision is not yours."

"But it's the wrong decision!" he burst out.

"Antimony, please. Show some respect."

"But you aren't listening."

"We *have* listened. You just don't like our decision. We can't rush into a major construction project for no reason, when there is so much to do here. We must consult the archives and learn what we can."

"But we need to do it now."

"Why, Antimony? *Why?*" His mother sounded impatient now, embarrassed at his rudeness before the high council.

"I…" Antimony faltered. "I don't know why. I just know it."

"Well, I'm afraid that's not enough." His mother's look softened. "I know this is important to you, but we can't risk dwarves' lives by sending them into an unknown place where they could be cut off with no way of returning."

There was a tense pause as Antimony glared at his mother and the other council members. They stood united, showing no sign of backing down. Antimony was outnumbered and outranked. There was nothing he could do. The high council had spoken.

Then, unexpectedly, a quiet voice spoke up from the hallway.

"I'll go."

9

MYTH OR MAJESTY?

Everyone turned to look at Zil. She blushed at the sudden attention, but returned their incredulous looks with a brave stare. She was hot with embarrassment, but her heart was beating with an excitement she had never felt before.

She had come to the doorway to peek in and see the portal the dwarves had discussed. She had heard Antimony's repeated attempts to convince the council of the mission he so clearly felt called to. She didn't know why, but his story and his request for the dwarves to go and restore the king's palace had struck a chord with her. For the first time since the destruction of the castle and her home, Zil saw a glimmer of hope in the hopelessness. For the first time since purpose had been robbed from her, she could sense a new purpose to reach for; a purpose that could be hers and hers alone.

Antimony's vision to restore the palace was quite possibly insane, but it had captured her imagination. If forgotten ruins could be restored to beauty again, perhaps other things could be too. Perhaps this broken kingdom or her own sorry-looking life might have hope and beauty once more.

She had nothing to lose and nowhere else to go. The portal offered a means of escape from the miserable situation she found herself in; to flee the places and people who had worked together to cause all the hurt she felt. Even more than that, it offered a fresh start in a place so removed from here that no one even knew where it was.

"I'll go," she repeated when no one said anything.

"And who are you?" one of the dwarfish councillors said, fixing her with a befuddled expression from beneath huge, red, bushy eyebrows.

"This is Zil, one of my guests. Is that right, dear?" said Opal.

Zil nodded.

"Zil dear, as you have heard, we don't know if the portal is safe. Our decision is that too much is unknown for us to risk sending someone through again."

"You wouldn't be sending me. I'm choosing to go. You said I was a guest here."

"Of course you are," said Opal with a worried smile.

"Then I am free to leave as and when I like. I'm not a dwarf, so I don't have to abide by your decision. There's nothing here for me any more. I want to go." She looked over at Antimony. "I want to see what he saw. I want to... to *do* something."

"That's all very well, but–" began the grey-bearded dwarf they called Granite, in a dismissive tone.

"Why are you all so afraid?" she demanded boldly.

"We're not afraid. We're being sensible and cautious," said Granite.

"You are doing nothing. That's exactly what you did before. *Nothing.* When our homes were being destroyed and our villagers enslaved, you talked about the king's justice but did nothing to bring it about. That's your problem. You're all talk and no action." Zil turned to face Opal. "Thank you for bringing me into your home. You have been kind and I am grateful, but I'm going to go."

Without a second thought, she squeezed her way into the room. Taken aback by her confidence, the councillors squashed themselves backwards, so she was able to make her way through the packed bedroom.

Antimony found himself pressed even more tightly against the wall of his room as the councillors made a narrow corridor for the fearless young woman. He watched her in awe. If only he could be half as brave! His attempts to stand up to the high council had been met with nothing but simple refusal, yet here was a young woman, a *human*, informing the dwarfish high council of her intention to go through the mirror.

His heart pounded in his chest. "I'm going too," he blurted.

"Antimony, you can't!" protested Opal.

"I've already been through and I was fine," he pointed out. "Besides, you're happy to let a human go. If I choose to go freely, why should you stop me?"

"Because you are a dwarf and we are the dwarfish high council."

"I'm sorry, Ma, but I need to do this."

"But Antimony, youre my son. I don't want anything to happen to you."

"It won't. Please trust me."

He could see she was torn between her trust in him, and her desire to protect him; torn between the council's decision and Antimony's plea.

"I'll come back tonight," he promised her. "I'll scout out the area and come straight back. You don't need to worry. We might even be able to work out where it is."

He fixed his ma with a pleading but determined look.

She pursed her lips. "You are old enough to make your own decisions, Antimony. You must do what you think best."

Antimony gave her one of his warmest smiles. Then, hurrying

in case any of the other council members decided to intervene, he grabbed his satchel from the hook on the wall, stuffed in a sketch pad and some charcoal, and squeezed his way through the crowd to stand with Zil in front of the doorway that led to the long-lost ruins.

Zil parted the curtain of vines and stepped through, looking around in amazement. Antimony followed close behind, feeling the tickly, web-like sensation of the cracks breaking over his skin. Then he was standing in the ancient quarry, with the sounds of the forest all around him and a cool breeze that felt refreshingly welcome after the crowded, stuffy cave. Behind him, the astonished council members peered through the gaps in the vines that hung across the strange door.

"Be careful! Come back immediately if there's any danger," his ma's voice called after him.

Neither he nor Zil replied. They were too busy drinking in the peaceful forest and the sense of adventure.

"Which way to the ruins?" Zil asked, her face lit up with excitement.

"This way. It was about one hundred and seventy steps from–"

"You counted?"

"Not specifically. My brain did though."

She gave him a strange look and started walking in the direction he had indicated.

Antimony would have quite liked to have told her in more detail about the number of steps to the ruins, but something in the way she had looked at him made him think better of it.

He started after her, recounting the details of his previous visit to the wood. She listened absently, looking around her with eager anticipation. Unconsciously, he counted the steps in his head as he led her toward the ruins. He always did; it happened without his even thinking about it.

They wove their way through the dense forest of ancient, twisted trees. There was nothing scary or threatening about the wood. It exuded a friendly, magical kind of presence that only added to the otherworldliness of the place. Antimony could almost believe the trees had been there since the beginning of time.

"…and over here I found a dragon's eye beneath the water."

"A *real* dragon's eye?" Zil's eyes widened.

"Not a real one; a carving with a huge gem. Look, it's on the bank there."

"It's beautiful!"

They paused for a moment to marvel at the dragon's eye. Antimony took the opportunity to examine his companion more closely. She still wore the same filthy clothes she had been wearing the night they brought her back from the ruined castle: a plain dress such as a servant might wear. He knew from their first meeting, when he had led her back to his home, that she had no other possessions. She had clearly tried to scrub the dirt and grime from the wretched clothes, but they were beyond cleaning. The fact that she had tried though was a sign of her determination. Her confidence made him feel a little nervous. It was as if she were an unpredictable animal, friendly for now but liable to become fierce and powerful in a moment.

She was clearly exhilarated by the adventure, full of life and energy. When he had first met her, she had been subdued and mistrustful, keeping herself to herself. The girl before him was like a different person.

"It's exactly what I would expect to see on a king's palace." She looked up triumphantly with an almost mischievous smile. "Isn't it strange to think that we may be the first people to see this in hundreds and hundreds of years?"

"At least that many," said Antimony, as they started walking again, crossing the small stream. "I haven't read much about the king, but one book mentioned that the great betrayal happened only forty years before the first high ruler of the dwarves was appointed. That was Great Potash himself. Great Potash ruled for forty years. His beard was thirty-one-and-a-quarter spans. After he died, Diamond the Delicate succeeded him. Her beard was twenty–"

"Why are you talking like that?" Zil interrupted. She had a habit of doing that.

"Like what?"

"All deep and slow."

"I'm reading," he explained.

"No, you're not."

"I am."

"You're not. I can see you're not. You don't have a book or anything." She gave him a suspicious look, as though she suspected he was playing a trick on her.

"I can see it in my mind. I read it six hundred and fifty-three days ago in the library. *Lavarock's History of the Dwarfish Nation.* Page twenty-six, I think."

"You think?"

"That's what it said, but there was a blank page at the beginning and I don't know if you're meant to count those."

She looked at him strangely again. "What was the great betrayal?" she asked after a brief pause.

"It was when the king's servants rose up against him, because they wanted his power for themselves. You must know about it."

"Hmmmmm. I think a minstrel sang about it once at the castle. Was the king actually real, then? Do you really believe in him?"

Antimony stopped and stared at her in amazement. "Of course he's real!"

"Really? I thought he was just another one of those old stories. I mean, my own mam told me about him when I was a kid, but she also said dwarves can shapeshift in the night and steal naughty children away. It turns out that's not true."

"She said *that*?" Antimony asked in amazement. How could the humans tell each other such strange tales and yet fail to know about the good king?

She shrugged. "I thought the king was just another one of the fables, like Evad the thunder knight or Roof the dragon-tamer."

"But you talked about the king's justice earlier," he said, still dumbfounded.

"Everyone talks about the king's justice," she said simply. "It's just what's right and wrong, isn't it? Anyway, I was just repeating back what your high council said."

Antimony looked at her in confusion. It had never occurred to him that others might not take the king's existence for granted. He knew plenty of dwarves who thought the king was long gone; a distant part of history, interesting but irrelevant. He hadn't dreamed people might question his very existence. But then human lives were shorter than dwarves'. They lived sixty or seventy years rather than two or three hundred. That probably meant they forgot the past more quickly.

"If there was no king, there would be no king's justice. Anyone could just do as they please and who would be able to say what was right or wrong?" he pointed out.

"People do behave exactly as they please," she responded matter-of-factly. "The lords and ladies wage war against each other. They let us ordinary folk die for the sake of moving a border a stone's throw in one direction or the other. The dwarves trample over anyone they like, to add more gold to their greedy pockets. The king's justice is always ignored, so perhaps there is no king."

"We don't... Well, maybe we did, but we are trying to change," Antimony replied defensively.

Zil was nothing like he had expected. Her mind was sharp, and she said things simply and to the point. It made him stop and think.

"Maybe if people who claimed there was a king lived out the king's justice, more people would believe that it's real," she said.

Antimony pondered on this, but couldn't think of anything else to say. He decided she was probably right.

"You're, er, different from most dwarves," Zil ventured after a short while, as they hit one hundred and thirty-three steps and approached the hill where the ruins were.

"I know, but my mother says she thinks my beard is due a growth spurt any day now."

"Really? Maybe that's it then." She gave him another of her odd glances.

One hundred and fifty-eight.

One hundred and fifty-nine.

They reached the tree line and stepped out into the large clearing where the palace mound was located. The line of rubble that marked the original position of the walls was just visible. The sky was overcast but still bright after the gloom of the canopy.

"Here we are. Just up this hill and you'll see it all. Then we can make our map."

10

STONE BY STONE

H_{mmmmmmm.}

Things were different. Sparks could tell. The time was coming. She was aware of something happening within her.

Awareness.

That was new. Was this what it was like?

Sparks didn't concern herself with it. It didn't matter. Not yet.

Soon, she thought. *Soon.*

They climbed the steep mound.

One hundred and sixty-nine.

One hundred and seventy.

One hundred and seventy-one.

That was odd, thought Antimony. It had been exactly one hundred and seventy last time, but sometimes that happened. It was close. Perhaps he had taken slightly smaller steps so that Zil could keep up with him.

They stood at the top of the hill beside the low line of rubble – all that remained of what had once been a towering whitewashed wall. He had reached one hundred and eighty-four steps. That meant he had taken fourteen extra. Fourteen would be… what was it? Just over eight per cent of his original one hundred and seventy, meaning he had adjusted each step by approximately…

"Antimony, I was talking to you!"

"What? Oh, sorry. What did you say?"

"I said you can see for miles from here. Do you think you could draw a map? I saw you grab some paper and charcoal."

"Oh yes. I could have drawn it at home, in fact."

"What?" Zil stopped sharply and put her hands on her hips. "Stop saying things that aren't true."

"I'm not!" he insisted. "I can remember things. That's… well… it's what I do. True, it will be easier now I'm here, but I could have drawn something fairly accurate."

"You're teasing me," she accused him. "Just because I was a serving girl doesn't mean I'm stupid, Antimony."

Her flash of anger startled Antimony, who certainly didn't think she was stupid. "I'm not. And I don't think… Why would you…?" Antimony struggled for the right words. What had he done to offend her?

"Can you really remember all that?" she asked with a frown, after he had failed to produce a coherent answer. Her anger seemed to have subsided as quickly as it had risen.

"Yes. I mean, I remember words and numbers best. I like numbers in particular, but I only saw it this morning, so I could probably remember the view well enough. It's simple enough to imagine it from above and turn that into a map."

"Is it?" She looked unconvinced. "I'm not sure I could. How would you do it?"

Antimony responded by reaching into his satchel and removing the parchment and charcoal. Taking them over to a nearby chunk of masonry, which he used as a table, he began to sketch while talking.

"We start with the palace mound here. It looks to be almost perfectly circular, which makes it easy. We'll put this right in the middle here." He drew a small circle in the middle of the paper. "I'll draw a more detailed map of the palace layout on the other side, when we've walked around a bit more. Now, the sun is over there, which means that mountain on the horizon over there is north. Can you see?"

Zil squinted to where he was pointing. "What? That dark smudge? How do you know how far away it is?"

"It was clearer this morning. The bad mist is thicker there now, so I don't really know how far it is. I suspect the scale will be a little inaccurate, but I can make a rough guess. For instance, over there – about thirteen degrees to the left of those hills, just before that bit of mist that looks like a wobbly pickaxe – I think that's a lake."

"Thirteen whats? Oh, wait. The bright thing?"

"Yes. That'll be the sun reflecting on the water. Anyway, it looks about half as distant as the mountain. If I mark both on the map it will give us a rough scale. Now I just have to compare any other landmarks we can see with these and we can get a rough idea of where things are in relation to each other."

"Oh, I think I understand. So what about those mountains there?" She pointed to a mountain range that stretched some distance.

"I'd say that's north-west, and roughly two-thirds of the distance to the lake."

He marked them on the map. They spent a while longer looking for other landmarks. The palace mound was positioned perfectly for the job, with panoramic views of a vast distance on three sides. They must be quite high up, thought Antimony – an excellent site for a castle or palace. Parts of the view were clear, but occasional clouds of yellow fog hung menacingly over the landscape like bulbous, tentacled creatures, obscuring whole sections.

The direction they had come from, back toward the quarry, was more difficult to map. The hills into which the quarry had been cut blocked that view, but Antimony hoped the other three directions would give them enough reference points to compare his map with the detailed maps in the dwarfish archives.

In a relatively short space of time they had created a basic map. There wasn't much to show for it, with a disappointingly large amount of empty parchment still on display. He noted down that this was mostly dense forest.

"When the fog moves, we can check for anything else that was hidden. We don't have much to go on at the moment." Antimony was looking at the simple map and scratching his head. All he could see was a few mountains and lakes, and lots and lots of forest. It could have been a map of almost anywhere in Presadia. "While we wait I'm going to try to map out a plan of the palace."

"Good idea," Zil agreed. "I'll start clearing the ruins."

She immediately rolled up what remained of her sleeves and bent down to pick up a piece of masonry. Lifting it with a grunt she placed it beside another piece.

"You'll what?" Antimony asked, puzzled.

"I'll start clearing away all this mess. We can reuse the stone, can't we? It'll be much easier to start work if it's not strewn all over the place. It's just like a messy dining table. You have to clear away all the untidiness and clutter before you can lay it all right again." She moved another brick and added it to her pile.

"Use the stone for what?"

"Rebuilding the palace, of course," she replied, as if he were stupid. "That's what we came here for, right?"

"Well, yes. But I thought you didn't even believe in the king? It's going to take you forever if you have to do it one stone at a time."

"How else do you build a palace? And I didn't say I didn't believe in the king. I just didn't say I *did*. You need to listen better."

Antimony stared at her. His new friend baffled him. She seemed to flit between emotions with greater speed than a runaway mine cart. She confused him, but at the same time he was intrigued. Already his brain was working out how many hundreds of years it would take a single woman to rebuild the palace. Yet, while he stood there doing nothing but thinking, she was already moving her third piece of rubble.

He couldn't object. He was the one who had been crazy enough to think they should rebuild a long-forgotten palace for a king who hadn't been seen in hundreds of years. He should be grateful he had found the one person crazy enough to try to rebuild it completely alone, and with nothing but her own bare hands.

"OK," he said, wishing he could think of something cleverer.

Leaving his peculiar new friend to her work, Antimony wandered about the top of the wide mound, sketching out how the palace must once have been. It didn't take long. The main outer wall ran in a circle around the perimeter of the hill. The area it enclosed had been spacious, a good one hundred and sixty paces across. Footprints of other buildings were still in evidence against the inside of the wall. Then there was a large area with no sign of foundations. Gardens perhaps? His vision had only shown him the view from the outside.

In the middle of the mound, a curious wall of huge, blackened stumps, with splintered tops like shattered teeth, surrounded a wide, circular patch of bare ground, devoid of grass or other plants. A smell of dead ash hung in the air. Something about the place made Antimony's skin crawl.

At first he thought the black stumps were stone, but on closer inspection he realized the blackness was the same sickness that had appeared on many of the trees in Presadia. It covered the stumps completely. If they were trees, they were like none he had ever seen before. Each trunk was almost three times wider than

80

the span of his arms, and as hard and cold as stone. They must have been long-dead, but showed no signs of rotting, despite the disease marks.

Antimony frowned. He was missing something. Where was the foundation for the middle building, the great twisted keep he had seen in the vision? He couldn't forget it. It was the most outlandish building he had ever seen.

The walls and foundations seemed to fit the vision perfectly. He knew, for instance, that the stone wall around the edge of the hill had been about three times his height and painted a brilliant white. In the sunlight, it would have shone brilliantly. It had a roofed walkway and four slender towers, each made from polished silver metal and topped with a spire of glittering colours. At the front were huge gates, also made of silver, which had the appearance of being part of the wall itself. When opened, it would have looked as though a large section of the circular wall had swung open.

The black stumps stood where the middle keep should have been. The elegant tower he had seen had been bone white, and taller by far than the surrounding walls. Somehow it had been constructed to resemble many strands, woven together and twisting up into the sky. It narrowed as it climbed, like a twisting ivory horn tipped with a jewelled spire. How *had* it been made? Could the tower have been constructed around the woven trunks of the great trees? How had someone grown them like this? Trees this size would have taken hundreds, maybe thousands, of years to grow. It was a mathematical conundrum beyond even Antimony's quick mind.

The strange combination of materials – the whitewashed stone, silver metal, bone-white wood and glittering gems – had puzzled Antimony. Each part seemed to celebrate its own individuality while, at the same time, the distinct sections melded together into a beautiful whole, like four distinct flavours combined in a delicious dish of food.

Next to the plan of the ruins as they now stood, Antimony sketched a rough version of the palace as seen in his vision. It took him a while, but when he was done he looked at the two side by side. They were barely recognizable as the same place. So much would need to be done.

He looked back at Zil, still methodically moving stones small enough for her to carry. A grassy space about the size of his bedroom was now clear of all but a larger chunk of masonry that Antimony guessed was too heavy for her. The patch was laughably small, but it was the first step.

He stood watching for a moment longer. Then, inspired by Zil's example – and in spite of the maths – he rolled up his sleeves and went to help.

11

THE USURPER

Opal waited in Antimony's bedroom long after the other council members had left. There was much she should have been doing. With High Lord Tin away, her stack of reports and requests was unusually large, and her human guests would need supper soon.

She sat on her stool considering her son. Antimony was becoming his own man. He was no longer a boy and – she hesitated to think it – no longer really a dwarf. He would always be her son, always her beloved, but he was growing up. She wanted to cling on to him, her little boy, her gift. Ever since that day in the abandoned tunnel when Copper had found him, she had wondered what or who had given them such a precious and wonderful gift. Where had he come from, and why had they been chosen to find him?

Now Opal wondered whether she had done a good job in raising him. Maybe she had clung too tightly to him. Perhaps she should have done things differently. Maybe they should have told him from an early age how he had come to be their son. Now the unspoken truth felt so huge and late in coming that Opal didn't even know how to start.

It was agonizing waiting for them to come back. She didn't know what she would do if the mirror portal were to disappear, but she couldn't tear herself away.

She had sat there long enough to see the light change. The overcast noon had given way to an evening bathed in pale sunlight. Dwarves were not too bothered about sunlight. Most burned quickly in the sunshine above ground, but sunlight had become rarer in Presadia. The sky had grown stormier, more brooding, and the yellow mists came more often, thicker and heavier. So now, the pale rays that filtered through the trees seemed particularly beautiful to Opal.

Presadia was dying. Only one hundred and sixty years ago, when she had accompanied the dwarfish trade caravans as a young guard, the trees had been greener, the water clearer and the sunshine warmer. There had been some of the tree sickness – the mists had appeared occasionally and some of the elderly or weak had suffered from the coughing sickness – but nothing compared with the way things were now. The great infirmary of Val-Chasar didn't just house the poor humans who had suffered in the wars; it was filled with dwarves who choked and spluttered from the coughing sickness brought on by the yellow fog.

She sat up as she saw movement across the clearing. Two figures were coming through the trees toward the portal. Her heart soared with relief.

Antimony had come home.

Antimony, Ma, the chief groomer, and an ancient librarian stood around the table in the map room of Val-Chasar's great library. It was late. Antimony stifled a yawn. The librarian shuffled across the shelf-lined room with incredibly slow steps, pulling out large leather tubes that contained dwarfish maps of Presadia. The librarian looked more ancient than any of the books, his skin as wrinkled as the craggy leather covers adorning the dusty volumes he cared for. Each time he pulled a tube from the square shelves, the action looked as though it might unbalance his bent and frail frame.

It had taken him a long time to gather the selection of maps on the large table around which they all waited. Unfortunately, many of the maps that showed the entirety of Presadia didn't offer much to compare with the landmarks on Antimony's hastily drawn map. There was plenty of detail around Val-Chasar and the places or routes the dwarves regularly travelled; those were easy to map out. Further afield, however, there were large sections on many of the maps that were almost entirely blank.

"Are we sure it's even in Presadia?" the chief groomer asked irritably. "The mist and tree sickness might have spread beyond the borders of our kingdom. We must have gone through a dozen or more maps."

"Only eleven," corrected Antimony.

"It could well be somewhere other than Presadia," Opal agreed, sounding tired, "but we need to start with what we know. Only once we have ruled out Presadia can we be sure that it's somewhere else. The fact that Antimony's drawing of the palace seems to match the legends and surviving descriptions makes me confident that this is in fact the location of the king's old palace."

"Here is one of the oldest maps in our collection. It's from before the disappearance of the king," the tiny librarian said, reverently placing a dark tube on the table. "It marks the Old King's Road and surrounding lands that used to connect up the entire kingdom."

"The King's Road?" Antimony said with renewed interest.

"Yes, parts of it are still in use. Our caravans travel along it to reach the human settlements: west toward the edge of the Great Forest and north right up to Stonebridge. The road within the Great Forest has become far too dangerous to travel and has fallen into disrepair. It was only really used to reach the Silverwood anyway, and the elves have made it clear they want little to do with dwarves and humans."

"Why is it dangerous?" Antimony asked.

"To begin with, it was just bandits. They preyed on any traveller foolish enough to walk those roads. Now there are few travellers, so the thieves are mostly gone. The greater danger in the forest is the Rebel Elf."

"The who?" Antimony asked.

"Oh, come now. If you are speaking about the so-called Usurper, everyone knows those tales are nothing more than exaggeration and superstition," the chief groomer scoffed.

"Don't be so quick to question your elders and betters," snapped the librarian with a strength that defied his old age and frail body. "Aye, it's him I speak of. The Rebel Elf, the Usurper, the Vengeful Servant, Kalithor the Vengeful. He has many names. Don't be so quick to reject the stories."

"I've read about the Usurper," said Antimony. "I didn't realize he was a rebel elf though."

"It's all rumours; nothing is proven," Opal put in quickly.

"Word has it," went on the librarian, speaking directly to Antimony, "that the Rebel Elf lord is holed up in the forest with his followers – all kinds of unsavoury creatures. We don't know for certain why he was banished from the Silverwood, or how big his army is. But he and the forest are best avoided.

"Legend has it that it was he who led the rebellion against the king, and he destroyed the palace you are looking for. He crushed all efforts to find and restore the king to his throne. Then came the wars, when he tried to take Presadia by force. But alas for him, too many others wanted the same thing. They tore each other's armies to shreds. That's when he withdrew to the Great Forest, some believe to gather a new army, capable of conquering the whole kingdom."

Carefully, he removed a flaking map from the tube and spread it flat on the table, using stones to pin down the edges. It was the most detailed of the maps they had seen, with many notable features and landmarks recorded in black ink, with descriptions written beside them. Unfortunately, there were singe marks along one edge and the bottom left-hand corner of the map was completely burned away.

"I didn't show you this one before as the damage is bad. But the detailing is exquisite." The librarian pointed to a mark on the map with a small inscription. "The Old King's Road connected Val-Chasar in the east with the Silverwood in the west. That would lie around here." He waved his hand at the missing corner of the map.

"It cut right through the heart of the Great Forest. As you can see, we are missing that part. You can see here, just at the edge of the burned section, how the road also went north to Stonebridge and the larger human towns."

The junction point had also been lost to the fire, but Antimony could follow the roads and imagine where they met before they continued west toward the Silverwood.

"Bad things have happened to travellers trying to reach the Silverwood via the King's Road. Those that do return tell terrible stories of half-men and mutated beasts. Many never return at all. People from the villages near the forest edge disappear without trace. The only folk who go there willingly are those attracted by the stories of the Usurper himself." He lowered his voice and leaned toward Antimony. "Rumour has it that he is building an army like no other. There is a force amassing in the Great Forest that will soon march out to claim Presadia for the Usurper."

"It's just a camp of villains and runaway criminals – nothing more," the chief groomer said, looking rather pale.

Opal nodded. "We don't know what's in there. It's silly to guess or get carried away with rumours and children's stories. The high council has been investigating these tales for some time and has found no clear evidence of any such army. It's true there have been reports of disappearances near the forest, but that could just as easily be wild beasts or people getting lost."

Antimony stared down at the Great Forest on the map, imagining a terrifying horde conquering Val-Chasar. It wasn't a pleasant feeling.

To the north of the burned section, a lake and mountain caught his eye. Scanning the area to the south-east, he saw a gap in the forest with large hills, marked on the map as little humps. Quickly, he scrabbled around for his own map. Yes, there it was: the mountain, the lake, the thick forest all about, and the hills. Antimony studied the position of the palace on his own map and worked out where it would have been on the burned one. There. Or at least it would have been there if the section hadn't been missing.

He stabbed a finger on the table, where the missing corner of the map should have been. "It's here. In the heart of the Great Forest, by the King's Road junction. The king's palace is right here!"

12

MANY HANDS

Zil couldn't wait to return. The ruined palace had cast a spell on her and she was entranced. The sense of adventure was intoxicating. Finally she felt free, making a decision all by herself; for once, not simply the victim of other people's actions. It might have looked crazy, even to her, but it was a craziness she had chosen.

She tossed and turned on the hard floor. Apparently, dwarves slept on solid stone. They had thought folded blankets would be more than comfortable enough for the humans, but they weren't. Yet it wasn't the hard floor that was keeping Zil awake; it was her racing mind. She couldn't stop thinking about the palace and the exciting new opportunity, so different from anything she had experienced in her broken and bitter past.

Antimony had insisted they come back to Val-Chasar for food and sleep, and to allow him to check his makeshift map against the dwarfish archives. She would happily have stayed, but once again her rumbling stomach had made the decision for her.

She had spent the evening telling the other refugees about the excitement of their discovery, and the mystery of the palace ruins.

She told them about Antimony's vision, describing in detail what the palace looked like and how he believed they could restore the ruins to glory. Some had thought she was making it up, but she had managed to convince a few to go with her in the morning and see the portal for themselves. Her mind was still buzzing with thoughts of the palace when she finally slipped into a sleep filled with twisted towers and glittering spires.

Someone was shaking Antimony. He opened his eyes, groggy and confused.

It took him a moment to realize where he was. It wasn't his bedroom, where the portal loomed like an open cave mouth. Instead, he was bedded down on the floor in the main living space, next to his new friend Zil. She had been fast asleep when he had returned late, after a long, dusty evening in the archives.

Zil was still shaking him. "Come on, Antimony. There's lots of work ahead of us and we won't rebuild the palace if you sleep all day."

He blinked, unaccustomed to so much noise first thing in the morning. Zil was more jittery than a cave crab: angry and stubborn one moment, excitable and enthusiastic the next. She had more enthusiasm for rebuilding the palace than he did. *Potash only knows why*, thought Antimony. She certainly wasn't as aware of how challenging rebuilding a palace was going to be. Even with a large team of trained dwarf masons it would be a major project. It would be quite impossible with only two of them, even if they worked at it for a hundred years.

"What time is it?" he asked with a yawn. Looking around the room, he saw that most of the refugees were still asleep. Ma wasn't at the stove preparing breakfast. It must be very early indeed.

Zil saw him looking over at the stove.

"Your ma has already left. She said there were fresh flatcakes for everyone in the oven and a basket of bat nuts on the table. I've never eaten a bat nut before. They don't taste very nice."

"Gone?" Antimony asked, still feeling groggy. "Gone where?" Where would his mother go at this time in the morning?

"She said something about the high council. I don't know. Are you coming? The others are already waiting. We've got food to bring with us, so you can eat at the palace."

"Others? What others?"

"Some of the folk staying here. And I went and spoke to some of the others I know from Lord Raven's castle and told them about the portal and the palace and, well, you'll see. They wanted to have a look. No one's got anything better to be doing. I said they can only come if they're happy to help clear the ruins."

"Oh, right," Antimony said uncertainly, awed by the fiery and decisive energy that propelled his new friend. He couldn't imagine what she had been like as a servant. Surely servants were meant to be quiet and submissive, and blend into the background. Antimony couldn't imagine Zil ever blending into the background. She created a kind of organized uproar wherever she went. Perhaps, he concluded, she had not been a very good servant.

Antimony allowed himself to be led to his bedroom, collecting his satchel of papers and charcoal, still yawning, and blinking the sleep from his eyes. The "others" turned out to be eight ragtag villagers, ranging from children to an elderly but spry-looking man. They had squeezed into the bedroom and were looking with interest at the mirror portal. Their murmuring stopped as Zil and Antimony entered.

Hardly a troop of dwarfish master masons, thought Antimony to himself.

Zil raced through some introductions with such speed that even Antimony couldn't keep track. Everyone seemed more concerned with passing through the magic portal than with light conversation.

Before Antimony knew what was happening, Zil had led the little party through the mirror.

Once on the other side, she led them at a brisk pace toward the palace mound. Antimony, a little more awake now, drew alongside her.

"Zil, who are these people again? I recognize a few who were staying with us, but half of them I've never seen in my life."

"I already told you. They're folk like me; people with nowhere better to go and nothing else to do. You dwarves made sure of that."

"I told you we—"

"I know, I know, you're trying to make amends. Well, while you do that, we're all more concerned with building new lives for ourselves. There doesn't seem to be many options on the table. Rebuilding a ruined palace in the middle of goodness knows where, for a king who hasn't been seen in hundreds of years, is turning out to be the best one." She gave him one of her cheeky grins.

Was this entire situation a game for her? Antimony could see a firm resolve in her eyes. Zil was focusing on the vision of the palace as strongly, perhaps even more strongly, than he was, only for different reasons that Antimony couldn't fully grasp.

"Breakfast?" She handed him a flatcake from the small shoulder bag she was carrying. Then, before Antimony could think of anything to say, she strode confidently ahead, raising her voice to explain where everything was, as if she had lived there all her life and was giving guests a guided tour.

When they reached the palace mound, she split them into two groups, with directions as to where they should start clearing and where to pile up the rubble that could be reused. Antimony let her take charge. It allowed him a moment of peace and quiet to gather his own thoughts. A few humans moving rocks was a start, but they had a lot more planning to do, and help would be needed if they were to rebuild the palace. Antimony found the rock he had used as a table the day before and pulled out his plan of the palace, as well as a fresh sheet of parchment for his calculations.

Basic pictures were all very well and good, but he would need proper dimensions to calculate the materials needed. He would have to consider how each part should be worked and how to use the small group most efficiently. With only nine people on board he would need to use mind over muscle.

The central keep – the centrepiece of the palace – was a mystery to Antimony. He would have to come back to that. He would start with the outer wall: a simple yet impressive structure of thick stone. The gate would also require more skill and resources than he had, so that would have to wait. It wasn't as if they needed to defend themselves from anyone.

This thought reminded Antimony of the librarian's stories of the evil elf, the Usurper, and the rumours that he was gathering an invading army. There was nothing at the palace hill to indicate that there was anyone else around. Hopefully, the tales were nothing more than rumours. Antimony and Zil had no soldiers or means of defence. The forest looked so vast and empty, a few people on top of a hill would hopefully go unnoticed.

He was so engrossed in his calculations that the hours slipped by in no time at all. His stone table was gradually covered with sheets of plans, detailed estimates of materials, tools needed for each job, and construction designs.

It was exhilarating. Antimony's brain felt like a tickled magma-worm, bright and pulsing, illuminating the dark path ahead and bringing order and direction to his mad plan.

It was some moments, therefore, before the movement at the forest's edge filtered into his awareness. With surprise he looked up from his workings. A huddle of humans was gaping and pointing up the slope. The original group was still working further along the flat-topped hill, unaware of the newcomers. He looked back along the woodland edge. Antimony counted quickly. There were thirty humans. Like the first group, they were all ages, and mostly in damaged or stained clothes that indicated a range of former professions. Some had buckets or bags containing provisions and blankets.

One of them, an older man, saw him and waved. The group began climbing the hill toward him. Not knowing what else to do, Antimony walked to the edge of the hill and waited for them.

"Hello. Are you the one they call Antimony?" The man had a confidence about him. He wore cracked leather armour and Antimony guessed he had once been a soldier. He seemed at ease with speaking on behalf of his shabby group.

"Yes," said Antimony. "Er… who are you?"

"I'm Luss. We've come to help."

"To *what*?"

"To help rebuild the king's palace. Zil's expecting us. Everyone's talking about it. Apparently, the king is coming back and we are to repair the palace. She said we had the chance to be part of a grand mission. I have to admit, I wasn't convinced until I saw the mirror portal, but now I've seen–"

"A grand mission?" Antimony repeated, bewildered.

"Yes. An opportunity for us to create a new life for ourselves, here in the enchanted forest," one of the spokesman's companions added, hope painted across her face.

"Sorry. Did you say *enchanted* forest?" Antimony asked incredulously. What rumours had been spreading among the human refugees in Val-Chasar? What had Zil been up to last night?

"Exactly," said Luss, as if Antimony had confirmed their point.

"So, what do you need us to do?" the hopeful woman asked.

The other villagers looked at Antimony with expressions of interest and expectation.

"Well…" Antimony hesitated, unused to giving orders, "…the others are over there, clearing the ruins so we can start work."

"Excellent. We'll go and help. Ilyda, Jooash, maybe you can get a fire going and make a camp to start cooking up some of that food you've brought. It's not long till noon." Luss looked to Antimony for confirmation.

Antimony nodded, not knowing what else to do. The man smiled in return before casting an impressed eye over Antimony's makeshift table and the parchments covered in complex calculations and lists.

"Excellent. Come on, everyone. Let's leave Master Antimony in peace. He's got important work to do."

And so the workforce grew. With almost forty people clearing the ruins, progress was much swifter. The palace mound took on the look and feel of a working camp. Some of the human helpers dug a firepit to stew apples and oats for a hearty midday meal. As the day crept on, more humans drifted into the camp with the dazed look of people who wondered if they were dreaming. In her whirlwind manner, Zil quickly put them to work, and by mid-afternoon there were half a dozen big mounds of reclaimed rubble, and a few makeshift shelters made from branches and tree boughs had been erected around the firepit.

The people had dived into their work with an enthusiasm and energy Antimony hadn't expected. They smiled and laughed, their new-found purpose distracting them from the horrors they had been through and the helplessness of sitting around in Val-Chasar. It was cheery and good-natured, and Antimony found himself smiling as the laughter and singing of the workers washed over him.

By nightfall, the low foundations of the main outer wall had been cleared back. They were about the height of his shins and looked solid still, despite their age. Antimony examined them with interest. With the rubble cleared, he could see the huge stone foundation blocks. He knew they would continue right down to the very bedrock. Whoever had done such a thorough job of destroying the castle above ground had not been able to destroy it below. Even in ruins, the palace had retained a secret, hidden strength that no amount of wickedness and malice could erase. It would save them a huge job. Having strong foundations already laid would save them months, maybe even years, of work.

As the final light faded, Antimony stood and looked out at the palace mound, amazed by all that had changed in less than a day. He hoped that tomorrow would be as good as this day had been.

For the first time, he felt as though they might actually be able to rebuild the ruins.

13

ATTACK

Opal stood outside the council chamber and stifled a yawn. It had been an early start. She had managed to race round and visit all the council members before they started their day's work and convince them to join her at the council chamber.

She thought back to the funny thing that had happened that morning. She had risen even before the first rays of light had kissed the lip of Val-Chasar's mighty chasm, in order to prepare enough food for breakfast. Humming under her breath so as not to wake Antimony and the others, she had thought about her plans and arguments as she rolled flatcake dough onto a metal oven tray. These moments of morning peace were precious.

As she picked up the tray of flatcakes, it had caught the light. For a fraction of a moment, Opal was sure she had seen a strange building mirrored in the metal. It had looked like a hazy reflection of the palace Antimony had described and drawn on his map. Had her mind played tricks on her? She blinked and tilted the tray back and forth, trying to make it happen again, but was distracted by a light knock at her door. She had quickly put the tray in the oven and turned her attention to the early visitor.

It had been a group of seven or eight humans, who looked sleepy but excited.

"Good morning. Can I help you?" Opal had asked in her friendliest manner, trying to cover her surprise.

They had shuffled about for a moment before a young woman was prodded forward to speak for them.

"Please, ma'am, we're here for Zil. She asked us to arrive early, like."

"Oh… Zil, did you say? I don't think she's even up yet. Do you mind waiting there for a moment? Let me wake her."

It was beyond Opal, what the villagers might want with Zil at that hour, but she had woken the young woman anyway. Zil had almost burst out of her bed in excitement.

"You mean, they actually came?" she squealed, causing others to stir in their sleep. She scrambled to her feet, smoothing down her crumpled dress.

It obviously wasn't strange for humans to visit each other at the crack of dawn, so Opal had left her to it, telling Zil to pass on instructions about breakfast, and explaining that she was visiting the council members to arrange another meeting.

Humans were strange folk – Zil even more than most. Opal wasn't yet sure what to make of the young human woman, but had been secretly impressed by her boldness in standing up to the dwarfish high council. Common sense told Opal that the mirror portal was an unknown and potentially dangerous thing. Antimony's fixation with rebuilding the palace could just be his imagination running away with itself. But there was something else – something inside her that ran deeper than common sense – that believed the portal was there for a reason. She knew her son better than he knew himself. She knew his fads and fascinations, but this was not one of them. She would have bet her beard that his vision was a true one. The other high council members might have considered caution the best option, but Opal felt the forgotten ruins calling her.

Now she had what she needed: a location. They had proved that the palace was in Presadia. Any dwarves sent to survey the palace or work on Antimony's project would not be lost in some other world with no way of getting back.

All she needed to do was convince the other council members.

Screams.

They echoed around the clearing and caused Antimony to lift his eyes from the calculations he was working on.

More screams.

Alarmed, he ran in the direction they were coming from. He was still clutching some of his papers, which he stuffed awkwardly into the large pocket in his trousers. Reaching the edge of the round hill he looked down to see the humans who had gone to collect water for the evening meal.

A group of oddly armoured men on great black warhorses rode among them, threatening to trample the poor people. The other workers had also heard the noise and joined Antimony.

The horsemen, seeing the gathering on the hill, turned their attention away from the terrified cooks.

"Who are ya, then?" one of the horsemen called out in a cruel, guttural voice.

He was the most hideous person Antimony had ever seen. Antimony suspected he might be human, but half his face was a pale green, with pockmarked scars that dribbled pus. The ear on his near side was hairy and pointed, like that of a badger or a wolf. There were crude dark stitches against the pale bald scalp where the ear had been sewn in place. It made Antimony feel sick. The other side of the man's head was covered in lank, thin hair that hung to his shoulders.

His companions were equally mutilated. One was clearly a dwarf, but his beard was cut unnaturally short, like a human's. The feet of small animals and birds were plaited into his beard, as if a hundred wretched creatures were trying to claw their way out. He was incredibly fat but looked no less dangerous for it. His armour was black, his helmet fashioned from a deer skull. Antlers rose above it, making him appear bigger than he was, an impression aided by his humongous steed.

The third, another human, wore a hooded cloak over his black leather armour. A large scar stretched across his face like a pained grimace. Spreading out from the scar, small black greasy feathers had been sewn into his face. He resembled a half-plucked blackbird, and his dark cruel eyes made him just as terrible as the others.

"I asked ya a question. Who are ya to trespass upon King Kalithor's lands?"

The workers cowered in terrified silence.

Kalithor. Antimony knew that name. A shiver passed through his tense body as he remembered the list of names the librarian had used to describe the fabled Usurper, the legendary Rebel Elf who had led the rebellion against the king.

"Answer me!" The man kicked his horse forward and grabbed a nearby villager with a gloved hand, drawing a rusty sword with the other. The man in his grasp whimpered with fear and looked up at Antimony, panic and pleading in his eyes.

"Please, don't hurt him!" Antimony blurted, amazed he was able to gather the words when he felt so petrified. "We... we don't mean any harm. We are here in peace."

"No one is permitted on King Kalithor's lands without his permission. And he don't give permission. Last time. *Who* are ya and *what* are ya doin' here?"

"We're builders from Val-Chasar. We–"

"You're liars! Val-Chasar is dwarves. You ain't no dwarves. You know what King Kalithor does with liars?"

"Promotes 'em," the fat dwarf chuckled.

The first man – the one with the wolf ear – spat at the dwarf.

"He kills 'em," Wolf-ear said, answering his own question. He pulled back the rusty blade, preparing to bring it down on the helpless villager.

At that moment, many things happened at once. Antimony and the other workers yelled in horror as the blade began to fall. There was a *thrung* sound, followed by a sharp smack. Wolf-ear's arm was thrown backwards as though it had received an almighty yet invisible slap. The blade spun from his hand and splashed into the stream as he stared with astonishment at the slender white arrow piercing his wrist. The motion threw his balance so far back that he let go of his hostage. As he tried to rebalance himself, his huge horse reared in surprise, throwing Wolf-ear unceremoniously from the saddle. He tumbled into the small stream in an undignified sprawl.

The other two riders drew their own weapons and swung their horses around, looking to see where the unexpected arrow had come from. There was a moment of confusion as Wolf-ear struggled to get himself back up. He was still looking with disbelief at the arrow, fury painted across his dripping face.

One by one, a dozen slight figures stepped out from along the tree line. They seemed almost to melt out of the forest itself. If it hadn't been for their movement Antimony was sure he would not have spotted them.

He had never seen anything like them before, but Antimony had read lots of books and he knew them instantly.

These were elves.

14

FRIEND OR FOE?

Hazel Crumpetbottom – she hated her name, but there was no use complaining, for that was what it was – leaned forward. All eyes were upon her. Her little audience was like soft clay before the potter.

Storytelling was an art, a true art. It wasn't just a case of remembering and repeating back the old tales; it was about knowing which story to tell and why. It was about preparing the people to receive it; creating the atmosphere and drawing them in with other familiar tales until they were ready for the true story. Only then was it about bringing the story to life through the telling of it.

It was a serious responsibility, and one that could be misused. The storyteller always held power over those who listened. If she was good at her craft, the audience might never know *how much* power she truly had over them. Hazel Crumpetbottom didn't take the responsibility lightly.

Few people knew how to do it properly nowadays, she mused. Most of the villages in the area didn't even have a wise woman any more, and she couldn't remember the last time she had heard tell of a proper travelling bard.

But it was of no matter. Even if everyone else had forgotten or abandoned the craft, Hazel Crumpetbottom would faithfully keep telling the old stories.

She needed them tonight. It had been a bad day. A very bad day. Another child had gone missing while collecting firewood: nine-year-old Elias. They had searched the edges of the Deepwood. All that night and most of the day they had looked, but he was gone without a trace.

The people of Wiggleswand crowded into the meeting hut, sad and tired, but in no mood to return to their homes. Wiggleswandians stuck together at times of crisis. As it had always been, so it would always be.

She looked at Gannapple, the missing boy's father, shuddering with near-silent sobs in the corner. It was uncomfortable to see such a huge, burly farmer reduced to uncontrollable tears.

She pursed her lips, sensing the mood.

The villagers were ready, she decided. Ready for the main story they needed to hear that night.

It had been a difficult decision, settling on the main story. It would be hard to tell and hard to hear. It wasn't a fantastic myth or a humorous legend set in a far-off kingdom. Tonight's story took place closer to home. It was known as "The Fall of Presadia", and the villagers had heard her tell it before. It was not a cheery story. Some might have wondered why she chose it when they were already feeling so down. However, Hazel Crumpetbottom knew that to foster hope, a storyteller had to be real about the bad things in the world and the hurt people felt. That was the power of hope: it shone even brighter in darkness. It was most potent when hopelessness appeared to be all-consuming.

She took a deep breath and struck a chord on her small harp. A chord of beginning. It would awaken a feeling of memory in her listeners, opening them up to the words she was about to say.

She looked up through watery eyes at the sombre faces of her little flock and began to sing.

The fat dwarf and the hooded man calculated their odds. They didn't need Antimony's mathematical brain to see that they were outnumbered and overpowered. Each elf held a slender, full-height longbow with an arrow aimed at the horsemen.

There was a long, tense pause, disturbed only by the grunts and splashes of Wolf-ear as he tried to regain his saddle without using his injured arm. Only when he had eventually remounted did one of the elves speak up.

"It is long past time you were gone, vermin of the rebel. Skulk back to your master."

Antimony watched, holding his breath. The three horsemen backed away from the stream edge, not daring to turn their backs on the elves.

Wolf-ear glared venomously at the elves and then at Antimony. Loathing seethed in his cold eyes.

"King Kalithor will hear about this," he hissed.

"He is no king of ours. There has only ever been one true king in Presadia. Your *master*" – the elf almost spat the word – "never truly knew him. Begone now, unless you wish to receive a matching arrow in your other hand."

The Usurper's minions needed no further urging. They swung their horses around and galloped into the forest. When the pounding of hooves had faded from earshot, the lead elf nodded at one of his silent archers, who melted back into the trees, presumably to ensure the horsemen didn't double back unexpectedly.

"Thank you." Antimony spoke up when the forest was silent once more, save for the chirping of the birds and the blowing of the wind. "You saved us. I… *we* thank you."

"You are fortunate. We came north to avoid the Rebel Elf's

stronghold. It blocks the King's Road. We had hoped to avoid contact with any of his vile followers. We came across them just before they stumbled on your camp. It was well for you, I think. But who *are* you?"

"We are from Val-Chasar – or at least I am," said Antimony.

"So you said to the others. But Val-Chasar is the home of dwarves, not humans."

"Yes, I'm a dwarf. These humans are from the villages around Val-Chasar. Our high lord decreed that we take in anyone who has become homeless or starving because of all the... the problems." Antimony fell quiet, unsettled by the elf's unreadable expression.

"It's true," Zil said, stepping forward. "The dwarves took us in, but we have come here instead. What... Sorry, I mean *who* are you?"

It struck Antimony that Zil and the other refugees would never have seen an elf. In truth, Antimony had never met one either, but he had read descriptions of them in the Val-Chasar library. Their semi-transparent skin took on the colours of the forest. This, combined with the complex tattoos that covered their bald heads, made them unmistakable.

They were shorter than he had anticipated, however. For some reason he had expected them to tower over him, perhaps because they were ancient and immortal. Some elves were as old as the kingdom, or so it was said. Perhaps, thought Antimony, it was simply because the author of the book in which he had read about elves would have been of usual dwarf height.

What had it been called? Oh yes, *Peoples and Creatures of the Presadian Realm* by Othoclase the Rocker. In his mind, Antimony skimmed the pages about elves, refreshing his memory.

Before the elf could answer Zil, Antimony bent over and pressed his palm flat against the earth.

"Greetings to you who share Sister Nature. I am Antimony of Val-Chasar."

The lead elf looked taken aback that Antimony knew the formal elven greeting. Nevertheless, he responded as appropriate. "And to you, fellow travellers over Brother Ground. I am Tommarind of the Silverwood." He looked Antimony up and down appraisingly. "It is unusual to meet one who knows our ways. I see you have been in the company of elves before."

Antimony blushed. "Well, no. Actually, I just read it in a book."

The elf nodded, but his expression was softer than before. "And what brings you all the way from Val-Chasar to the depths of the Great Forest, and only a stone's throw from the Rebel Elf's den?"

"A stone's throw? We didn't know he was there." Antimony frowned in concern. "It's a long story. In short, we have come to rebuild the king's palace."

"Really? So you *do* know the significance of this place. I thought it had passed away from the memory of dwarves and humans by now. But I would like to hear the story and the connection you have to Val-Chasar. We are heading there ourselves to demand justice from the dwarfish high council. This palace is many days' travel from there."

"The high council? Why do you want to see them?"

"Just yesterday, their high lord stormed into the Silverwood with a fearsome dragon. They kidnapped our queen! We have travelled through the night, barely stopping. We are heading to Val-Chasar to demand Queen Ellenair's return, and justice for this heinous crime."

"High Lord Tin kidnapped your queen?"

"Indeed! They claimed to be on a foolish quest to find the long-lost king. Queen Ellenair told them of the fruitlessness of their mission. When she refused to help, High Lord Tin's dragon snatched her up and made off with her. We don't know where they have taken her, but we suspect some dwarfish scheming. Perhaps they wish to demand a ransom to further line their treasury. Such is the shamefulness of the dwarves these days…"

"Oh no, that's definitely not it. High Lord Tin would never do that! Anyway, Khoree the dragon does not belong to High Lord Tin or *any* person," insisted Antimony, wondering what sort of trouble Tin had got himself into. "But they really *are* looking for the king. He's the only one who can get Summer and Jonah home."

"Summer and Jonah? You know of the children? How do you know of this quest to kidnap our queen? Are dwarves and humans scheming together now?" Tommarind suddenly became guarded and suspicious.

"There really was no quest to kidnap your queen. I'm as amazed as you are that it happened. I was there when the high lord took the children to visit Khoree for her advice. I saw them fly off to the Silverwood, but they only wanted advice. They hoped you would help them find out where the king was. Khoree, the dragon, believes he is still alive somewhere." Antimony's words tumbled out. "I really don't know why they took your queen, but Khoree has quite a temper. If she decided to do it, I'm not sure Tin or the children – or anyone – could have convinced her otherwise."

"Who are you to have been present for such things? And since when do dwarves and humans keep such tight company?"

"I was part of the group that first encountered the children and brought them back to Val-Chasar. My mother is on the high council, and High Lord Tin is my mother's brother's wife's fourth cousin. We're very close. As for these humans here, their homes were destroyed in the recent wars. They are refugees with nowhere else to go."

Antimony explained how the children had been the pebbles that had started an avalanche of change in Val-Chasar, and how High Lord Tin had commanded that the human refugees be welcomed in. One thing led to another and Antimony found himself explaining the story of the magic mirror and his vision to restore the palace.

The elves let him speak uninterrupted, their faces impossible to read. As he spoke, Antimony realized the humans were also listening in rapt silence. Of course, they probably hadn't heard the full story either.

"So here we are. I'm the only dwarf, but these humans have been arriving all day to help."

"You are a dwarf?" Tommarind sounded surprised. "And you have arrived through a magic portal to restore a palace that's been in ruins for over seven hundred years?"

Antimony nodded. "I can show you the portal if you like. I'm sure the high council would talk to you and explain how the whole situation with your queen is just a big misunderstanding."

The elf stared at Antimony a moment longer. "Your story is too strange and far-fetched to be a lie. I fear it is nothing more than the ravings of a madman." He looked at Antimony carefully. "But perhaps you speak the truth. Take us to this 'portal' and we shall see."

15

AMBUSH

Hazel Crumpetbottom's husky voice and clear harp filled the small meeting hall:

> *"Back before the days of dark,*
> *Before all evil made its mark,*
> *In peace Presadia flourished bright,*
> *No shadow but the cool of night.*
> *The king upon his silver chair,*
> *Reigning just and ruling fair,*
> *Belov'd and cherished, as deserved,*
> *His favour poured out unreserved."*

There were more verses about the beauty of Presadia as it had once been. Her aged voice filled the little room, painting colourful pictures of an unblemished kingdom.

She could have cut some verses, but after a hopeless day, Hazel Crumpetbottom wanted to remind the villagers that their world was not all bad. No matter how dark and dreadful it looked, it had once been fair and perfect. Their world was not inherently bad. It was a beautiful thing that had simply become broken.

> *"But then there came an evil night,*
> *From which began the kingdom's plight.*
> *Some simple whispered words, that's all,*
> *Which started fair Presadia's fall.*
> *A royal servant, noble elf,*
> *One chosen by the king himself,*
> *In whom a seed of envy grew,*
> *Which twisted what was good and true.*
>
> *'This king who sits upon that throne,*
> *Why should he all Presadia own?*
> *And who's to say we wouldn't be*
> *Far better were we truly free?*
> *For I believe that if we willed,*
> *We'd do as well, or better still.*
> *Let's make ourselves now our own lords,*
> *And take the power that this king hoards.'"*

Hazel Crumpetbottom sang about how the elf's whispers had tempted others with stories of the power and wealth that could be theirs; how he had flattered and convinced them that they were just as good, wise, and capable as the king himself; how they had become full of pride, resenting the king; how they had joined in the elf's secret plot to overthrow him.

> *"Through palace halls the rebels swept.*
> *Upon his throne, the good king wept*
> *For friendship broken, love betrayed;*
> *For broken oaths and hearts that strayed.*

They beat upon the throne room door,
To kill the king they'd served before.
But there within no king was found,
Just shattered mirrored glass around."

The song didn't tell where the king had gone, and Hazel Crumpetbottom suspected this was because no one really knew. Some thought he had been killed by the rebels; others believed he had escaped. The song did tell of the chaos that followed. The rebels had turned against one another, each believing they should take the king's place. Some had died, while others had escaped to raise armies to take Presadia by force.

The palace had been burned and broken. Devastation had washed over the land. From that first betrayal, cracks soon spread. Before long, they had swallowed Presadia. The armies had destroyed each other. The few pitiful survivors slunk away into the shadows: the dragons to who-knew-where, the dwarves to Val-Chasar, the elves to the Silverwood, and the humans to continue fighting over the lands in between.

It was a dark story, with verse after verse of hopelessness. But that wasn't the end.

"Then silence fell, like final breath,
Presadia choked in blood and death,
A shattered land by terrors haunted:
The 'freedom' that the rebels wanted.
They'd turned against their one true king,
And by their actions everything
They once had owned was now destroyed,
Instead of joy, a hopeless void."

Hazel Crumpetbottom let a sad chord ring through the small room.

She paused until it had faded into silence, then continued without the harp, the sudden absence of music lending unexpected power to her words.

> *"But do not fear and do not weep,*
> *Presadia will wake from sleep.*
> *She'll rise from ashes, live again,*
> *Be healed from all her hurt and pain.*
> *For though he left, we know not where,*
> *Presadia still has her heir,*
> *And though she's broken, still she yearns,*
> *In waiting till her king returns."*

❦

Antimony was nervous leading the elves toward the quarry and the magic portal. What if the portal had decided to vanish? The elves would think him either completely mad or a liar.

He breathed a sigh of relief. There it was: the doorway through the cliff into Antimony's room, cloaked with its curtain of vines and the web of silver cracks. It glowed, casting a little aura of light around the empty quarry. Sparks must be awake. In fact, there seemed to be movement and activity behind the curtain. Was that the sound of horses?

Panic hit. Antimony imagined Wolf-ear and his accomplices ransacking his home and attacking his mother.

A dreadful sound seemed to confirm his worst fears: a familiar voice crying out. His blood froze. It was his mother shrieking. He had to protect her!

Tommarind shouted something as Antimony broke into a run. At the same moment, a horse burst through the portal's curtain and into the glade. Antimony threw himself aside from the rearing hooves just in time. In horror, he looked up at the formidable sight of a fully armoured rider and…

"Great beard of Boron, you stupid animal!" Ma shouted at her terrified pony. "You scared the life out of me, rearing up like that. I almost came off, you great ball of tangled hair!"

"Ma!"

"What? Oh, Antimony. What are you doing down there? I was coming through to find you, but this chasm-crow of a creature would *not* be convinced to go through the portal. Salt thought a mighty slap on the bottom might help – I mean the horse's bottom before you say anything. Anyway, I hadn't expected it to leap quite so suddenly. I remember now why I never ride these silly things. They are much better at pulling carts."

"Why *are* you riding it? What are you doing here?"

"What does it look like I'm doing here? I'm coming to help. It's been some years since I've ridden out in full armour at the head of a column of dwarves, but the council insisted that if I believed so strongly that we need to assist in this hare-brained scheme of yours I should lead the dwarfish contingent myself. The ponies really aren't practical, but apparently it's proper. I'd forgotten how uncomfortable armour is."

Antimony stared at her in amazement. He had never seen his mother in her splendid military attire. He knew she had been a chief among the dwarfish warriors when she was younger, but she had given that up when she married his father, before Antimony was even born.

It was a spectacular sight. Her armour was polished bronze and shone like gold. Pale opal stones, her namesake, studded the breastplate. On her head was a bronze skullcap. She had wrapped her beard around her like a scarf, as was common with dwarves when they travelled. Her long-haired pony wore matching armour and sported a large, comfortable saddle. In truth, the ponies really were much better at pulling carts, but this one certainly looked the part, and Opal was the image of a glorious heroine from the legends. Or a flustered, complaining heroine at any rate.

Another pony leapt haphazardly through the portal behind his mother, its rider whooping in excitement. "Onward, faithful steed!"

It was Salt, also in armour. Although ornate, it looked almost plain next to that of Antimony's shining mother. A line of other dwarves followed on foot, spilling out into the clearing and lining up in ranks.

"Ma, I was coming to find you. I need to–"

There was a thrum followed by a thump. An arrow embedded itself in the grass only a hair's breadth from where Antimony was standing.

"Halt your troops! What is this treachery?" Tommarind's concealed voice boomed. Antimony scanned the trees, but the elves had all vanished from view.

Opal spun her pony around to identify her enemy. She drew a battleaxe from the strap on her saddle.

"To arms! We are under attack!" she bellowed.

The dwarves became a clattering, clanging mass of confusion as they set about grabbing their weapons, awkward in their heavy armour and bumping into each other in their tightly packed column.

"Bows at the ready!" Tommarind's voice called out.

Antimony scrambled to his feet and ran toward the elves, or at least to where they had last been. He caught a slight movement and saw a bow being raised. The movement revealed the elf, who had stepped back into the edge of the forest, his camouflaged skin and natural stealth making him near-invisible.

"Stop! Everyone stop!" he cried.

"Antimony, come back! We have been ambushed," bellowed Opal.

"No, you haven't. It's the elves. Put away your weapons!"

"It is an enemy. They shot at us."

"It's all a misunderstanding. Please, Ma."

She looked at him and made a swift decision. "Halt! Dwarves, lower your weapons. Halt, I said."

The confused dwarves had only just managed to equip themselves with a random array of exotic weaponry, ranging from golden scythes and curved scimitars, to chunky maces and decorated lances. Now they all tried to lower them at the same time. Antimony winced at the cacophony of bangs and scraping of metal on metal.

"Please, Tommarind, there's nothing to worry about. This is my mother. I told you about her."

"You have led us into an ambush," said Tommarind.

"No, no. I didn't know there would be dwarfish soldiers – honestly. Anyway, they are not here to attack you. They're here to…" His brow creased into a baffled frown. "Why *are* you here, Ma?"

Opal, who still couldn't see where the mysterious voice had come from, spoke at an unnaturally loud volume.

"I am Opal Oval-Axe, member of the dwarfish high council. I have been sent with my fellow dwarves, soldiers, and masons to help Antimony in the restoration of the king's palace. We come armed, believing there may be a camp of villains and dangerous criminals nearby. We come to ensure safety for the humans and dwarves working here, in case the magic portal should suddenly vanish."

"This is the portal of which you spoke?" asked Tommarind's voice.

Antimony nodded. "Yes. I didn't know that Ma – sorry, Opal, erm, Oval-Axe – was coming. But now they're here, please put away your bows so we can all talk."

After a pause, Tommarind stepped out from his hiding place among the trees.

There were murmurs of astonishment from the dwarves. Only a few had seen an elf before.

"I am Tommarind of the Silverwood. We journey to Val-Chasar to speak with the high council. Since you are here, I would be willing to speak with you directly as a council member."

"Of course, of course," Opal replied, quickly regaining her composure. "I am pleased to meet you, Tommarind. What matter brings you all the way from the Silverwood to speak with us?"

"I come to demand the return of our kidnapped queen, stolen away by your high lord."

Opal's mouth dropped open.

16

THE SILVER HANDPRINT

What under earth had that silly, excitable fool Tin got them all into now? Kidnapping the elven queen? What was he thinking? It was hardly the behaviour of a high lord!

Opal had been at a loss as to what to say. She had suggested they go to the palace hill to discuss everything. She wanted to see the ruins for herself, but also needed time to think about the unexpected accusation and give Antimony a chance to fill her in on what had happened.

"Attacked, you say? Do you think it was this Usurper fellow?"

Antimony nodded.

"Oh dear, our fears are confirmed then. It seems I was too late. Thank the depths those elves arrived when they did. But tell me, do you know anything else about this supposed kidnapping?"

"Not much, Ma. It sounds as if Khoree the dragon grabbed the queen. I tried to tell them that dragons don't answer to dwarves, but they're pretty upset."

"They have every right to be," said Opal. "I can understand now why they were so jumpy about us. I knew nothing about this

117

kidnapping. We haven't heard hide nor beard-hair from High Lord Tin since you saw them fly off."

They reached the hill and started climbing. Opal paused at the top to admire the site. There were several large piles of rubble and exposed foundations where walls and buildings had once stood. Near one side the humans had made a camp kitchen and were eating a hot broth that smelled delicious. At the centre there was some kind of blackened henge, a wide circle of huge, ominous black stumps.

"Let's head over there and talk in private," said Opal to Tommarind and Antimony. "Salt, can you organize the supplies and tents? Make sure there are always a couple of good dwarves guarding the portal and a few lookouts up here. Tommarind, your elves must be tired and hungry from their journey. Let them rest and eat while we talk."

Tommarind spoke a few quiet words to his elves, who cast suspicious glances at the dwarves. He looked at the black stumps with a grim expression, but followed Opal and Antimony regardless.

"This is a bad place, Opal Oval-Axe. Much evil was done here," said Tommarind.

"Just Opal, please," said Opal. "Evil has been done here, certainly. But a bad place? It was the king's palace before any evil happened. We can't call this a bad place – only a good place that has been desecrated and spoiled; a good place that has been corrupted by evil, but a good place nonetheless."

Tommarind looked at her with new-found respect. "Well spoken, dwarf. I am young among the elves, but I remember visiting the king's palace before the evil that caused its destruction. Perhaps you are right. But the fact that it was once good makes the bad that has ruined it all the worse."

"We are restoring it," Antimony put in quickly. "That's why we're here. I saw how it should look in a vision and… well, I just knew we were meant to fix it."

"Magic portals, visions, dwarves and humans working together?" Tommarind shook his head. "Your story is a strange one."

"Yes, we agree." Ma laughed. "In truth, the high council members are as wary as you, Tommarind. But I believe Antimony's vision, and the magic portal speaks for itself."

"Perhaps." The elf was subdued as they neared the centre of the mound and the great blackened ring where once the keep would have stood. Antimony looked across at him and was surprised to see tears in the elf's eyes.

"I had heard of this," said Tommarind softly. "The mighty trees were once the centrepiece of the palace: twelve Great Silvers grown especially for the purpose, and woven together. It was perhaps the most beautiful building ever built by the elves."

"Wait. You say elves built the keep? That explains it. I've never seen anything like it before," Antimony said.

Of course. The books he had read told of the elves' magical connection with all that grows; how they could persuade trees and plants to grow where and how they wanted. Antimony had been astounded by the idea when he first read it.

"You have seen the keep? How? Another of your books?"

"No, I saw it in the vision." Antimony scrabbled through the papers stuffed into his pocket. He found his drawing of the palace and smoothed it out. "Here it is. I drew it just as I saw it."

The elf sucked in his breath, his eyes widening in recognition. "An excellent likeness. It is just as I remember." A sadness crossed his face as he lifted his eyes from the picture to the reality of what remained. The shattered and diseased stumps before them radiated gloom and death.

"When the wicked servants led by that filthy rebel sought to overthrow the king, they burned the great keep, scorching it with dragon fire."

"Khoree told us. She told us they taunted and mocked her until she breathed fire in her anger. She said she had burned the palace and that she could never forgive herself."

"Khoree? The same dragon you claim kidnapped our queen? She has much to answer for!"

"It wasn't her fault. She got angry, yes, but she has regretted it for hundreds and hundreds of years ever since. She never meant to burn the palace; she was tricked. Now she's trying to make amends."

"But burn it she did," Tommarind said bitterly, "and now the cursed sickness that plagues Presadia has covered even the little that remains."

He reached out a hand, placing it on the nearest stump, and closed his eyes. His brow furrowed in concentration. Antimony and Opal watched, wondering what he was doing.

Slowly – so slowly that Antimony wondered if he was imagining it – the blackness crept back from the elf's hand and a faint silver glow encircled his palm. Tommarind pulled back his hand and let out an exhausted sigh. His forehead glistened with sweat as he turned back to face Antimony and Opal, leaving a silver handprint on the diseased trunk.

"There is still life here, deep within the tree. It is almost worse than death to have your life so crushed and weakened, strangled by disease and destruction. This tree should be noble and strong, but instead it is broken and mournful. I have never felt anything like the sadness of this tree."

"Trees have feelings?" Antimony asked, interested.

"Not in the way you or I do, but they are living things with a purpose."

Antimony looked at the shattered stump with a new reverence. "Can they grow again?"

Tommarind gave him a curious look. "Perhaps. It would take many elves and lots of effort. Our magic is gentle. We do not command or force nature to do our will. We negotiate and encourage. The trees would need to work against the unnatural damage and disease. I don't know if they can do that."

"Would you try?" Antimony pressed hopefully.

"I am here on a different mission," Tommarind told him. "I seek the return of our queen."

"But we don't have her. I've already told you that."

The elf looked at Antimony for a long moment. "I find myself believing you, Antimony, but I am under orders."

"What Antimony has told you is true. I swear on my own beard as a member of the high council that we know nothing of your missing queen. If High Lord Tin is to blame, as you believe, we will surrender him to you for trial when he returns."

Tommarind considered this for a moment. "I am intrigued by this mission of yours. I believe it to be a good and noble one. I do not pretend to understand these visions and portals, but it seems something greater is happening here. Thank you, Councillor Opal; thank you, Antimony. I will send two of my elves to deliver your explanation and bring word from our people. In the meantime, the rest of us will stay here and see what can be done."

17

THE GREAT SILVERS

Sparks wriggled in her lantern. Not that she knew it was a lantern.

So small, she thought.

Real thoughts now. She was having more and more of them. She was growing. She was hungry.

Not long now.

The kind one had not been back for some time, but others had been there. Lots of others. Noise and movement. Lots of it.

She didn't care. She didn't really care about anything. Thoughts and caring were different. Perhaps she cared about him though. The kind one. She... felt something for him.

Hmmmmmm. Feelings. These were also new. Like thoughts but... more fiery.

Sparks wriggled again, thinking about her feelings and feeling her thoughts for the first time.

Word had spread that there would be elven magic happening. Dwarves and humans gathered around the elves. The light of a few torches pushed back the darkness of the night. The blackened stumps hunched menacingly in the gloom. Tommarind's silver handprint still glowed on one, seeming to suck the light inside it.

Ma stood solemnly on Antimony's left, maintaining her regal status. Zil fidgeted beside him, stretching on tiptoes to see what Tommarind and the elves were doing. Everyone was silent with expectation.

The silence made Antimony realize how noisy it had become with so many people around. The human contingent had swelled to almost sixty people of various ages. Antimony's last count had made it fifty-seven, but others were still drifting in as the story of the palace spread through Val-Chasar.

Ma had brought two hundred dwarves with her. Antimony had almost fallen over in shock. What she had said to convince the high council to send such a large number was beyond him. He would need to revisit his plans to take account of the generous workforce he now had at his disposal. Things would move much faster. Dwarves had a well-earned reputation for hard work, and an almost legendary skill in building and crafting.

The display of magic wasn't quite what Antimony or the crowd had expected. The elves, huddled together around the stump with the silver print, placed their hands on the surface and closed their eyes. Then they appeared to do nothing.

For a long time they simply stood, eyes closed. The crowd began to fidget and mutter among themselves.

"When are they going to do the magic?" Zil whispered to Antimony.

"I think they already are," he whispered back.

She looked disappointed. "I thought it would be more, you know, *magical.*"

Antimony wasn't sure what to say to that. Secretly, he was disappointed too, but he turned back to watch. The minutes passed slowly. Around him, the gathered group continued to shuffle and whisper among themselves. It was hard to see much in the dim light of a few torches, but he thought he could make out faint silvery outlines around the elves' hands. Underneath them, the black coating on the diseased tree was bubbling very gently, like hot tar.

Zil yawned loudly beside him. Ma stifled a yawn of her own. It had been a very busy day.

After a little while, Ma said, "It looks as if they could be here a while. I think I'll go and check how Salt got on with organizing the tents and pavilions, and then turn in. I was up very early today and could sleep through a cave-in."

"Yeah, I'm zonked," Zil agreed. "Antimony said you brought tents for everyone."

"Yes, although we might need more tomorrow if people keep coming. You can sleep in my pavilion, Zil dear. There's plenty of room. Are you coming, Antimony?"

He shook his head. "I'm going to wait here a while longer."

Opal and Zil wandered away, chatting softly in the dark night. He watched them as they headed toward the brightly lit pavilions that made up the now sizeable camp. It almost filled what would have been the palace gardens and went around the full circle of the wall. Everyone had kept their distance from the blackened trees, however. There was something uncomfortable about them.

From above, thought Antimony, the camp would look like circles within circles: the dark forest, the circular glade, the round hill with its ruined outer wall. Inside the wall were the tents, a ring of light surrounding the darker centre where the desecrated Silvers formed their own patch of circular darkness.

Wheels within wheels.

Antimony stood almost at the very centre, both physically and metaphorically. Somehow, all this had sprung up from nothing and Antimony seemed to be right in the thick of it. People looked to him to make decisions and lead the project. Even Ma had come to help him in his mission. How had it all happened? Surely they would all realize their mistake soon enough. He wasn't some wise leader. He was having to make it up as he went along!

He looked around him. Most of the people had gone, and the camp beyond the dark centre was jostling and noisy. Here, where he remained with a handful of others, it was quiet and still. Despite the busy camp, despite his fears and feelings of inadequacy and the inevitable challenges the next day would bring, Antimony felt oddly at peace in that moment. He sat down to remember the elves' gentle magic.

The night had been overcast, but for a moment the clouds broke and bathed the palace mount in the silvery radiance of a full moon, illuminating what he had not been able to see before. Around each elvish hand, the stump glowed with a growing patch of brightness, as if the moonlight itself were filling the tree, coating the scaly blackness with its own unblemished silver, smooth and fresh and new.

Antimony remembered what Tommarind had said about how the life remained, deep down in the trees. Their strength was hidden, but it was still there. No amount of damage had been able to destroy their spirits, much as the hidden foundations of the palace had remained strong despite everything above ground being utterly destroyed.

Antimony felt hope rising within him too.

He awoke some time later. In the clouded night it was hard to tell how long he had dozed off for. He was the only person still near the group of elves. The camp was quiet and calm, save a few magma-worm lanterns illuminating the occasional tent. He should go to bed, he told himself. He needed to be up early to organize the workers, and he still needed to update his calculations and plans to make best use of everyone who had come to help. He stood up to stretch. The elves were murmuring to each other, no longer working their magic. They looked exhausted.

The tree they had been working on looked healthy and new, a single silver stump in a ring of black. Approaching the elves, though, Antimony saw that this healing had come at a cost. The elves were not simply exhausted; they looked sick and pale. A few coughed painfully, and Antimony was dismayed to see black scarring, like the tree disease, on their skin.

Tommarind was struggling to keep his eyes open. One side of his face had turned an ash grey. "Antimony," he said, with a tired smile.

"Tommarind. How went the magic? It's been hours."

"Difficult. Ideally, we would have had more elves. The sickness runs deep and is old. The life spirit of the tree was weak. We have banished the sickness – that is the hardest part – but it will take more time and magic to grow it again into what it once was. And this is only the first of twelve."

"You don't look well, Tommarind." Antimony frowned with concern at the elf's ashen face.

Tommarind gave a weary nod. "We are asking the tree to do something that requires much energy. That energy has to come from somewhere. We do not resent the trees for taking it from us. To be able to help is always worth the personal cost. These trees are as much a part of creation as we are. We share in their pain and their damage, and we willingly take some of it upon ourselves."

"I never realized it would cost you so much."

"It has always been the way. Persuading a healthy tree to grow a little differently from its natural course does not require a lot of effort. The tree does not much mind if its branches grow to the left or to the right. But when we force the tree to do something it cannot do on its own, there is a cost. This tree was not made to fight off such a sickness." Tommarind breathed a heavy sigh. "Nothing in nature was."

They stood for a moment looking at the fresh, pale bark of the tree, glowing with a faint silver light in the near darkness. Antimony thought back to mending the mirror, and to his current project of restoring the palace. Building good out of bad wasn't easy, but Tommarind and the elves had shown Antimony that it was all worthwhile.

18

THE MUSIC OF THE MASONS

Zil awoke, excited. She wasn't the only one in the camp feeling that way. Despite the early hour there was a buzz of anticipation as people rose to see what the new day would bring.

So many people! Dwarves, elves, and humans all together, like… well, like nothing Zil had ever seen or heard about. It just didn't happen. She had only heard about elves in stories and never dreamed she would see them for herself.

Despite their differences, everyone was chatting and eating their morning meal together in a spirit of cheerful camaraderie. There was a sense of hope that was more than just the beginning of a new day. Zil wasn't the only one for whom the palace represented a fresh start. Many of the other humans had suffered the same sense of despair and helplessness after the destruction of their homes and lives. The palace offered them a purpose and a new home, at least for as long as the rebuilding took. She had no idea how long that would be.

The few elves who were up and about looked grey and exhausted, but at least they were no longer stiffly suspicious, as they had been the day before.

The dwarves, bemused at being sent to the palace, were nevertheless used to following the orders of their high council. Despite Zil's reservations, she was starting to see that they were a cheerful and good-humoured bunch, and she was beginning to understand how they might have been so oblivious for so long to the suffering their greed had caused. It hadn't been a malicious act. Being with them, she had come to realize that many had simply been unaware of the exploitation behind their comfortable lives. They had been used to a luxurious and privileged society, where wealth seemed to flow effortlessly. The majority had never been away from Val-Chasar and its maze of connected tunnels, and something about being distant and removed made it easier to ignore the things they preferred not to hear. Zil had heard about the two children from another land who had challenged the dwarfish high lord about the way they were behaving. But it sounded as though it wasn't until the refugees had actually started arriving on their doorsteps that all the dwarves had been forced to confront the uncomfortable truth behind their own comfortable lives.

Anyway, it was good to have more help for the task ahead. Rebuilding the palace might be hard work, but Zil found herself itching to get back to it. They had cleared a considerable amount of the rubble yesterday, and the foundations would soon be ready for the proper work to begin.

Rolling up the tattered sleeves of her threadbare dress, she marched her way over to the firepit for some breakfast. Perhaps Antimony would be there and she could find out what they needed to do next.

Antimony had come to his stone table early. He was determined to make the most of every person there. Many hands wouldn't necessarily make light work if they weren't properly organized. Efficiency was key. Antimony liked efficiency.

His papers were spread out, weighed down with odd bits of rock. He wanted to work out the production line. These lines were one of the secrets of the dwarves' remarkable productivity and efficiency: many people working in a chain together, but each responsible for one part of the whole, and for doing their part as effectively as they could. That way everyone could get really good at doing one thing, rather than needing to learn to do everything. Of course, it was only a part of their success. Dwarves were also imbued with natural ability when it came to making and crafting. It was in their blood.

First, decided Antimony, he needed to get the quarry working again. Any dwarf worth his salt had basic experience as a miner, quarry-dwarf or mason, and Ma had brought the finest with her.

While the quarry-dwarves started cutting great blocks of stone, and the stonecutters chiselled them down to a useable size, another team of humans and dwarves would clear a road up to the palace mound and build a bridge over the small stream. Then that group would be responsible for moving the great stone blocks from the quarry to the hill. Thank Potash it was only a short distance! Getting them up the slope would be the hardest part, but Ma had brought thirty of the strong mining ponies.

He considered the mess his bedroom must be in after hundreds of people – not to mention thirty ponies! – had passed through it. That reminded him: he needed to fetch Sparks. He would visit the quarry later, return to his room, and bring her back to his pavilion. It would be good to have some company that wasn't always asking him questions and expecting him to be some grand leader.

Once the stones were atop the mound he would need a third team to position them on the foundations. A fourth group would mix up the mortar to hold it all together. Two more groups remained: those who had taken to looking after the camp and cooking the food, and those his ma needed in order to watch out for any reappearance of the Usurper's troops.

He fiddled with the numbers in each group for a while, calculating things like stone size and how he could organize people into shifts to allow rest time. He enjoyed this kind of task. It was as if his brain were glowing, with numbers and ideas pouring through it almost too quickly to write them down. *This* was what he had been made for.

After a while he was happy with his plans. He rolled up his papers and followed his nose to grab some of the delicious-smelling breakfast from the cooking fire near his tent. Tommarind and a few of his elves were already there, with Ma and Salt. The black scars on their ashen skin seemed to have faded a little in the morning light, but the elves still looked exhausted, with dark shadows under their eyes. Antimony felt a surge of pleasure at the sight of dwarves, elves, and humans mingling so companionably over their food.

Salt spotted him and said, "Good morning, Antimony, my boy. Get yourself a plate of this most scrumptious breakfast. I've never tasted anything so delicious. If this is how humans eat all the time, I'm tempted to become one."

"There you are, Antimony," Ma chipped in. "I've set guards on each side of the hill to watch the forest and the quarry. I've also got two small groups doing regular patrols deeper in the forest, just to be safe. I've told the other dwarves to remain alert and keep their weapons near to hand, just in case. Now the Usurper knows we're here, I worry that we might receive more of his attention."

Antimony nodded, glad she was handling the military side of things. He wouldn't have known where to start with organizing guards and soldiers.

Tommarind smiled at him. "Good day to you, Antimony. My messengers have left to take word back to the Silverwood. I have asked that more elves join us here to see if we can restore all the Great Silvers."

Zil bounded up in her usual whirlwind manner. "Antimony, now we've cleared the rubble, what do you want…"

"Your ma mentioned you might need a team of dwarves to…"

"Can I request that the area around the Great Silvers is kept clear so…"

Antimony frowned, trying to listen to each person and form an answer, but with everyone talking at once it was impossible. It made his head hurt.

"Everyone, please be quiet!" he finally burst out.

The group fell silent and everyone looked sheepish.

"Now." He took a breath and turned first to his mother. "Ma, thank you for organizing the guards. Let's put them on four-hour watches and keep switching them so they stay alert and rested. You mentioned we had some master masons and quarry-dwarves. I'd rather not use them for guard duty. I think we should make the most of their skills. There might be soldiers among the humans, though.

"Tommarind, I hope your people decide to help us. You have already achieved things no dwarves or humans could do. I will make sure the central area around the stumps is clear and that you have everything you need. Zil, Salt, I'll be letting everyone know what they need to do in a moment. I'd like you each to find two or three people you think would be good at leading a team of people. I want them, and the rest of you, to meet me here in ten minutes. Has everyone got that?"

They all nodded. Antimony wondered if they felt as unsure about receiving orders from him as he felt giving them. Beard of Boron! He was ordering his own mother around. None of them questioned him, though. It was as if they all assumed he was their natural leader. How could he tell them he didn't feel at all certain he was the best one for the job?

His friends and his mother stood up to go about their errands before the meeting.

"Oh," Antimony added, "and Salt, the breakfast *does* smell delicious. I intend to eat some right away."

Antimony's bedroom really was a mess. It didn't even feel like his bedroom any more. Most of his things had already been taken to his pavilion. The bare room now felt like an entrance hall. The floor was filthy with the footprints of everyone who had passed through, and he wrinkled his nose at a pile of pony poo in the corner. It was still a hive of activity, however. Dwarves passed back and forth, bringing through new supplies, tools, and building materials.

He wasn't sure who was organizing the workforce this side of the mirror, but he made a mental note to write a list of what was needed. Ma had organized carpenters to reinforce Antimony's bedroom door and it was now several inches thicker than before, banded with iron and studded with huge square nails. Their main living room had been converted into a guardroom, to prevent any of the Usurper's men from wandering unchecked into the heart of Val-Chasar.

The only familiar thing about the room was Sparks' lantern, which still hung by the door. Antimony reached up and took it down, replacing it with an ordinary oil lamp.

He opened her lantern door. Strange. She looked even bigger than the last time he looked at her. He hadn't known magma-worms could grow so quickly. She would need a bigger lantern soon.

She was awake but dull, not too bright to look at. He thought for a moment that she was looking back at him, even though he knew it had to be his imagination. Magma-worms didn't look at people. They didn't even have eyes. He closed the door again and headed back through the portal.

A large team of dwarves, split into smaller groups as per Antimony's plans, had cleared away the foliage and moss from the quarry sides and were already cutting blocks, as tall and as wide as a dwarf. Antimony was immensely grateful for the quarry. Having a ready supply of stone so close to the palace would make the rebuilding a relatively straightforward task.

The first great stone was already being shaped by the masons. This would be loaded onto sledges for the ponies to pull up the hill. Antimony would have preferred wagons, but they would not fit through his bedroom door. In time, they could build wagons, though. The quarry-dwarves and masons sang one of the old dwarfish mining chants as they worked, the clatter and clacks of their tools beating in time to the rhythm.

> *"We'll crick and crick, and then we'll crack,*
> *We'll chip and chip, and then we'll chock,*
> *Through igneous stone, from magma hot,*
> *Through sedimentary layered rock,*
>
> *We'll hammer, hammer, then we'll stop*
> *To chisel, chisel, chisel, chop,*
> *Through metamorphic ribbon rock,*
> *To find our stony treasure crop."*

He smiled. The song was one used to teach children the different types of rock that could be found in the mines, but many grown-up dwarves still liked to sing it. Humming along, Antimony left them and strode toward the mound, stopping to call a few words of encouragement to a team laying split logs across the ditch and stream to form a bridge.

The palace mound was also a hive of activity. A mobile forge had been set up, and a blacksmith was hammering away noisily as she worked on the list of tools Antimony had given her. Adults and children crawled around in the foundations, chipping away at old mortar and removing weeds, ready for the new stone.

Laughter and singing filled the camp. Antimony had insisted everyone have regular breaks. The humans were not used to this dwarfish practice and viewed it as a holiday. It was another of the secrets of the dwarves' extraordinary productivity. To enjoy life they had to enjoy work, and to enjoy work they had to enjoy life. For the dwarves, time off was as important as time spent working. Workers who were well rested and relaxed were more effective in their labour.

In spite of their weariness, the elves were plying their magic on another of the stumps. The tree that had been cleansed the night before shone brightly in the daylight. Its top was still splintered, but fresh sap oozed from the stump. That was a good sign, according to Tommarind.

Antimony continued on to his workbench. He hoped that by nightfall the first stones would be mortared into place on the foundations. There would still be much to do, but everyone would be able to see the difference and feel encouraged.

Antimony reached the chunk of masonry he had come to think of as his workbench. He removed his satchel and took out his sketch of the palace. Although he had drawn it only days earlier, it felt as if years had passed; as if that had been another life. So much was changing. He had never expected the swell of people or the weight of responsibility. It had all just happened.

He ran his hands through his hair. As long as progress continued this smoothly, everything would be all right.

19

RAID

Mmmmm. Back with the kind one.

Something deep within her felt as though she knew him in a closer way. He was more than just the one who fed her. There was a connection. A name?

An... Ant...

The thought eluded her.

No matter.

Work had gone even more quickly than Antimony could have hoped. It was still true that one dwarf was worth two or three humans when it came to productivity, but the human workers had done an admirable job in matching the dwarves' enthusiasm. A good-natured competition had emerged as they tried to outdo each other.

"You only mortared twenty stones? Ha! I shaped more than ten times your weight in stone before noon. If it hadn't been for my chisel breaking, it might have been double."

"Chiselling stone isn't that hard, dwarf. You should try cooking for three hundred people."

The dwarf gave a big belly laugh. "You win. Even if I could, no one would want to eat it."

Antimony was pleased about the banter, even if he didn't understand it much himself. Light-hearted teasing confused him. Why couldn't people just say what they meant? However, it seemed to lighten the mood for everyone, so it made him happy.

The elves were still withdrawn, but this was due to their complete exhaustion and the effects of their magic. Tommarind looked almost skeletal. Large areas of his skin were dark grey and flaking. He coughed regularly. Antimony had wanted to wait for more elves to arrive before starting work on the other trees, but once Tommarind's mind was made up, there was no delaying him. The more time the elves spent with the Great Silvers, the more they felt their hurt, and the more their hearts ached for the sad, sick trees.

With night setting in, Antimony fetched Sparks' lantern so he could examine the day's work. She had almost become too heavy to carry and was eating far more than any magma-worm he had known before. He must remember to check with Ma if that was normal.

He started with a survey of the wall. In just three days most of the wall had reached his shoulder. It had risen far more quickly than he had hoped or dreamed. The closeness of the quarry and the abundance of help was making light work of the wall.

Scaffolding had been constructed around the entire inside length, with a big ramp near the gap where the gate would one day be. The fresh stones with their new mortar looked clean and bright, but between the new stones, older rubble had been reused to fill gaps, giving the wall a speckled look. One day, it would be plastered and whitewashed to match the palace of his vision.

He climbed up onto the scaffolding and walked along the edge of the wall. It was a cool night. The forest was wrapped in smudgy grey fog that stretched ghostly fingers toward the new wall. Antimony didn't like the fog. No one in Presadia did. Everyone knew how it caused the coughing sickness and made their skin itch. There was more of it about these days than there had been when Antimony was younger. His ma and the high council were always discussing it.

A dwarf guard waved a greeting. "Evening, Antimony."

"Evening," replied Antimony, wondering how everyone in the camp seemed to know his name. "Thick fog tonight."

The sentry didn't reply, but spun around to look at the forest. Antimony thought he heard someone stifle a cough.

"Did you—"

"Shhh," the guard replied in a whisper, his eyes scanning the fog-cloaked forest.

"Is anyone down by the quarry?"

"Just the portal guards."

"Perhaps someone's coming through the portal."

"Perhaps." The sentry sounded uncertain.

They stood for a moment longer, eyes and ears straining in the darkness. From the forest came the unmistakable sound of a horse whinnying.

"Horsemen!" the sentry said, with alarm in his eyes. "Horsemen! We are under attack!" he cried at the top of his voice.

He whipped a horn from his belt and blew three short, sharp bursts. There was a shout from the forest and then the sound of hooves picking up speed. Red torches bloomed beneath the trees.

One, two, five, a dozen.

Before Antimony knew what was happening, horsemen were galloping from the trees, crossing the grass in seconds and starting up the hill toward the opening in the wall where the gate would one day be. The two guards standing in the gap looked around in terror, unsure as to whether to hold their ground or run. Other wall sentries sprinted toward them.

The laughter and music in the camp died instantly as people reacted to the commotion. There was a moment of uncertainty, then chaos broke out.

People rushed for shelter, screaming and shouting, and tried to gather up terrified children. The dwarves, elves, and humans who had weapons rushed to their tents to grab them, but they had been caught off guard and weren't quick enough.

The horsemen had been slowed by the hill, but their powerful mounts were still eating up the distance alarmingly quickly. Antimony guessed at twenty-five attackers, but the fog and the speed of the horses made it hard to judge.

Not knowing what else to do, Antimony grabbed a loose stone from the wall and threw it at one of the raiders. It missed by a long distance. He had never been good at throwing. His second attempt was better, more from luck than judgment, but the small stone bounced harmlessly off the rider's black breastplate.

The dwarf beside him was struggling to line up a crossbow, a new dwarfish invention that was better than bow and arrow for short dwarfish arms. Finally he finished loading and released an arrow into the stampede below. Antimony had no idea if he actually hit anyone.

As the riders came nearer, Antimony saw Wolf-ear at the head, bent over his horse, slapping it viciously with the butt of his spear to make it move faster. His face was a snarl of hatred as he headed for the workers' camp.

The horsemen thundered through the gap and into the camp. They broke over it like a black wave. Makeshift benches were overturned, blades slashed at canvas and sliced through tent supports. Burning torches set the fluttering fabric ablaze. Within moments, the camp was dancing with an evil red glow, casting elongated shadows of frantic people and monstrous horsemen onto the new wall, which, rather than protecting them, now hemmed in the desperate workers.

People ran in every direction. Screams and shouts of fear, the pummelling of horses' hooves, and the sounds of ugly destruction merged into an overwhelming cacophony of terror. Flames leapt from tent to tent. Still the horsemen rampaged through the camp, overturning benches and tables, and slashing at anything in their path.

For several moments, Antimony gaped in frozen horror. Then he unfroze. He jumped down from the wall, still with Sparks' lantern in his hand. He had no idea what he could do amid such chaos, but he couldn't just stand and watch the people – his people – being slaughtered.

Ahead of him, one of the Usurper's troops had cornered a mother with a baby, and she was laughing at the poor woman's terror. There were no teeth in her mouth. Instead, yellow and black with decay, they had been woven into her long plaits. The teeth jiggled as she laughed, seeming to cackle with her like tiny skulls.

The rider raised her weapon, a crude club of wood and long animal teeth. Antimony yelled, his mind calculating how long it would take him to reach the helpless mother.

Five paces. Could he make it?

Four. The club was held high.

Three. The mother stared in horror as the club descended.

Two. Antimony bellowed wordlessly as he bore down on the rider.

One.

He made a final leap and swung the only weapon he had – the lantern. It smashed against the rider's arm, forcing her swing wide. The panes of coloured glass shattered, and Sparks exploded into a ball of brilliant light.

There was a hiss as the burning magma-worm hit the rider. Antimony closed his eyes against the blazing brightness and collided with the flank of the horse. It was like running into a wall. The horse whinnied and danced and stamped its foot, its rider toppling from the saddle to the ground. There she writhed desperately, trying to shield her eyes from Sparks' blinding light. Antimony squinted, pressing his face into the rough, sweaty neck of the horse. The mother was clutching her baby in one arm and covering her eyes with the other as she clambered to her feet and fled.

Antimony would have followed, but found himself jerked back, his arm caught in the horse's reins. Still blinded, he struggled to untangle himself. Then, with a flash of inspiration, he grabbed a firm hold of the leather reins and hauled himself up onto the great horse. It was more of a scramble than a dignified mount, the animal was so huge. He had only ever ridden the small dwarfish ponies before, and they were really too small for Antimony's long body and gangly legs. This was different. This monster was a warhorse for humans, and once he was in the saddle, the ground seemed a long way below him.

The horse wasn't bothered by the noise, the chaos or the fire, or even the change of rider. What did bother it, however, was Sparks' lightning brightness, and it didn't need Antimony to tell it to turn and head away from the felled rider.

Antimony blinked tears from his eyes and realized he couldn't see a thing. He clung blindly to the reins, trusting the horse while he waited for his vision to return. Sparks would have to wait. He would come back for her when she was cool and dim.

The size and strength of his new mount alarmed Antimony. He clung on for dear life as the horse made its own way through the ruins of the camp. Gradually, blurry shapes began to appear – running people, silhouetted against the dancing brightness of the burning pavilions. Only minutes had passed since the start of the raid, but as Antimony's eyes readjusted and his sight returned, the hilltop was already an unrecognizable battlefield.

Ahead of him, a familiar voice shouted.

"Ma!" he called, kicking the horse to a gallop.

20

THE FIRE

"To me! To me!" Opal bellowed, raising her battleaxe high.

She was cursing herself for the inadequate organization of their defences. There should have been more guards. She should have guessed something like this would happen. She should have pushed for Antimony to make the gate a priority. She should have...

There was little point in dwelling on past mistakes. There had been so much going on and too many jobs to be done.

"Tommarind, over here!"

Bow in hand, the grave-looking elf ran toward her. The more experienced warriors and soldiers, humans as well as dwarves, had gathered their wits and their weapons, and were starting to mount a defence. The enemy had only penetrated the first hundred paces or so of the camp, but had left total devastation in their wake. From what Opal could tell, it was only a raiding party and not a full-blown attack. Thank Potash's beard! It was small consolation, however.

Seven of her dwarfish warriors and a handful of humans were with her already. She could see others, alone or in small groups, engaging the horsemen. It seemed, though, that the Usurper's troops hadn't come to fight – simply to cause as much fear and damage as they could.

"Everyone follow me," commanded Opal. "We'll sweep around to the left and attack that big cluster of the enemy there."

She led her war band forward.

Tommarind ran beside her, swift and light on his feet despite his ashen appearance. His eyes were sharp with focus and discipline. As he ran, he loaded and loosed arrows without slowing. Opal was impressed.

Ahead, a gigantic black stallion galloped across their path. Tommarind raised his bow, then lowered it again.

"By the bush! It's your son. It's Antimony."

Sure enough, Antimony charged through the smoke and flames like a hero straight out of the old legends. Astride the huge warhorse, he looked tall and imposing. And, thought Opal with an aching heart, less like a dwarf than ever.

"Ma!" he shouted, catching sight of her.

She waved and gestured toward the enemy.

Antimony slowed and turned his horse clumsily to trot alongside her group. He was unarmed, so she pulled her back-up axe from behind her and passed it to him. It was only small, but Antimony had never been able to manage the heavy battleaxes anyway.

By the time they reached the enemy, there was little fighting to be had. The horsemen had been busy setting fire to anything that would burn, but pulled back when Opal and her troops approached. They were led by a savage man with a mangy wolf's ear stitched badly to the side of his head. Her stomach tightened. This must be the man Antimony had told her about.

Wolf-ear had seen them. He signalled to his troops to stay back. The workers had pulled themselves together and were organizing a robust counter-attack. Wolf-ear wasn't inclined to fight fairly.

"Leave now!" Antimony bellowed from his stallion.

Opal looked up at him in amazement. He towered over her, commanding and bold. Her quirky son? The boy who had always been so timid and gentle?

Tommarind strung his last arrow and aimed it at Wolf-ear. Opal saw that, instead of loosing it immediately, he looked to Antimony for approval. Even the elves were deferring to Antimony's lead.

Opal had a moment of uncomfortable realization. Antimony had become more than her awkward son. He was no longer a boy. Before her rode a man, a leader. One of those rare individuals that others were willing to follow.

"Leave now!" Antimony shouted again. All his anger at what had happened was vented through this single command. The strength of it took him by surprise. It cut through the clamour and was amplified by the walls that encircled them.

Wolf-ear had drawn back with his horsemen, interested not in a fair battle, but only in terrorizing defenceless workers. That made Antimony sick to the pit of his stomach.

How dare they? How could they? All the work and effort his people had poured in; the bonds of friendship that had grown up between the three races; the beacon of hope that this place had become for more than a hundred refugees. These wolves had desecrated it. They had laughed and jeered, as if destroying it were some kind of sport. The injustice burned hot in Antimony's veins.

He kicked his horse forward, gesturing with his arm for the others to stay where they were.

"Leave now, or fight us fair and square," he said.

Wolf-ear sneered. He prodded his own horse forward. Antimony was suddenly aware of how vulnerable his position was. His friends seemed a long way back. He didn't know how to make the horse walk backwards and he certainly didn't want to turn his back on Wolf-ear.

Wolf-ear carried a spear in his left hand. His right arm was bandaged where the arrow had wounded him the last time they had met. The wound was wrapped in filthy wolf's fur, to match his ugly ear.

"Oh look, the boy has returned. You've been busy; I'm almost impressed. But I warned ya, boy. This is Kalithor's land. You were told to get out." He was only a couple of paces from Antimony now. "I figured ya'd got the message, but it seems not."

Without warning, he launched himself forward, thrusting his spear at Antimony. Desperately, Antimony swung his axe to block the move. It was a wild and uncontrolled motion, but with Wolf-ear confined to his weak arm, his attack was not as powerful as Antimony had feared.

Their weapons connected, knocking Antimony's axe aside. As Wolf-ear's momentum carried him past, the axe slid down the shaft of the spear and, by complete accident, clipped the man's human ear. With his enemy now behind him, Antimony turned and kicked his horse to gallop back to his own people.

Wolf-ear reared up and howled, more in anger than pain. He raised his bandaged hand to the side of his head, staring in disbelief at the blood now dribbling down his face. Scarlet with rage, he looked wildly between Antimony and his troops, humiliated and furious.

Antimony, fearing he might attack again, was grateful to be safely among his friends once more.

"Shall I take him down, Antimony?" Tommarind asked quietly.

"Only if he comes at us."

Wolf-ear glared at Antimony, his face twitching in fury as he decided whether to attack. He spat at them venomously. "You'll regret that, boy! Next time it won't just be ya tents I burn. I'll be burning ya dead bodies."

He gave Antimony a final hate-filled glare before turning his horse and galloping toward the gap in the wall. He signalled to his soldiers, who followed him out of the smouldering camp and back into the dark fog of the forest.

"You have made yourself a true enemy, Antimony," Tommarind said. "Why wouldn't you let me take him out?"

"I won't sink to their level. We are better than them. They are filled with hatred."

"You may be right, but I fear that we might live to regret your decision. You saw what they did. This is war. Perhaps it is not a time for mercy."

"If only there had been more mercy in Presadia we might not be in such a mess now," said Opal. "We should never regret a right decision, even if it's a hard one that may bring further trouble on us."

Tommarind considered her words before bowing and nodding.

Antimony looked around him, assessing the situation. The enemy had gone, but fire raged through their camp. Even where they stood, smouldering embers and small fires smoked and burned around them. A burning upright from a tent frame collapsed nearby. Further away, the fire was still spreading.

A few people were dashing about, trying to tackle the flames, throwing buckets of water over the unburned scaffolding in an attempt to prevent it catching alight. But it was only a handful of workers and they were being careful not to waste a drop of the water, as if it were a precious resource. Others were hastily clearing tents from the path of the flames to create a firebreak.

"Why aren't there more buckets?" asked Opal in exasperation.

"There's no well," said Antimony. "The water has to be brought up from the stream. We've only been bringing up what we strictly need."

Why hadn't he thought of this and made better arrangements?

"Come on," he said. "Let's go and help."

By the time the flames had died down, almost two-thirds of the camp had been destroyed. Antimony had had to organize the dismantling of large sections of the scaffolding and the removal of dozens of tents to create an empty space where there was no fuel for the fire. After that, there was nothing to be done but to stand and watch the remainder of the camp burn, unable to do anything to stop it. It had been a long, demoralizing vigil.

Antimony wasn't the only one who felt devastated. This project had become a beacon of hope and a new home for the refugees. As for the dwarves, even though they were only there on the command of the high council, none of them liked to see their hard work destroyed. Antimony had heard more than one muttered complaint from dwarves who wanted only to return to Val-Chasar now his silly project had failed so spectacularly.

No one had come to speak with Antimony face to face. They all gave him looks: some pitying, others worried, and many accusing, but they left him alone to watch the flames and list the numbers – the losses – over and over in his head.

One dwarf.

Three humans, including one child.

Six ponies.

Seventy-two tents.

Three-fifths of the scaffolding.

Antimony wished his brain would shut up. He wished it wouldn't keep calculating the damage or pinpointing what could have been done if only he had been a better leader. But his brain never stopped. He hated it.

"Antimony." Ma touched his arm lightly, but he ignored her. "Antimony, the people are growing restless. I think you need to talk to them before things get ugly."

"What?"

"A lot of people are angry and upset. I think you should speak to them."

Antimony had heard the rising tide of complaints and squabbles breaking out. He looked at the quarrelling people. Nearby, a woman was accusing the dwarves of not keeping a close enough watch. A resentful dwarf replied that they would much rather have been at home in Val-Chasar than risking themselves for a stupid human project. Arguing was turning into shouting, the dwarves and humans growing increasingly angry with each other. The elves clustered together, watching the others with haughty detachment.

Antimony felt detached too. Alone. And useless. Completely useless.

"Antimony?" Ma pressed.

"What? Why me?" he snapped angrily.

"Because you're the leader here."

"No, I'm not. I'm a terrible leader. I don't know why I've ended up in charge. I never wanted this."

"Sometimes that's how it goes with leadership," his mother snapped back. "It's not all about us and what we want. True leaders serve their people whether they want to or not. Now is when your leadership will really count. I'm not sure the people will listen to anyone else." She paused and drew a deep breath. "I've never been prouder of you than in these last few days, Antimony. I only wish your father could have been here to see it."

Tears stung Antimony's eyes. He wished his pa was there too. Fathers sorted everything out. They made everything right. They knew what to do. Antimony didn't. He had no idea what to do or say. He wanted to run away from everything. The disappointment, the anger, the responsibility. He didn't want any of it.

But a deeper part of him knew that Ma was right.

He stepped out into the strip of barren ground that had been the buffer between the raging fire and what remained of the camp. He walked toward the embers of the still-smouldering tents. By chance, they had ended up near the great chunk of ancient masonry he had used as his table when he drew his plans and made his calculations.

He climbed onto it and looked at the grumbling, exhausted crowd he was here to lead.

A hush fell as the people saw him. Hundreds of faces. He saw expressions of despair, hopelessness, anger. The worst were the faces that were simply blank; devoid of all emotion; afraid to put any more hope in anything lest it be destroyed yet again.

They all looked at Antimony to see how he would fix this mess.

21

THE DEEPWOOD

Finally. Warmth.

Mmmmmmm.

Warmth was good.

This was what Sparks had longed for. She hadn't known she had longed for anything before now, but now she understood that this was what she had been made for.

So long in cold. So long asleep.

As the heat grew, so did her awareness.

She could feel herself awakening. *It was time. Finally. After... how long?* She didn't know. She didn't even know how she knew that it was time. But it was.

She wriggled deeper into the warmth. She let it soak into her body; felt it flow like slow, rolling waves breaking over her. As she absorbed the tantalizing heat she felt herself growing stronger and more powerful, sensed herself starting to change. Her own inner inferno mingled with the heat from outside, and bloomed in response.

She grew sleepy as she bathed in the blissful warmth. The space around her was hardening into a cosy nest, pupal sweat mixing with the hot ash.

She let herself sink into a deep sleep. Not the ignorant sleep of unawareness she had experienced before. No, this sleep was different. When she awoke from this sleep, things would never be the same again.

Antimony looked down on the angry and fearful faces. Distinct spaces had appeared between the groups of humans and dwarves. The elves waited, quiet and detached, watching Antimony with stern faces.

"I…" Antimony spoke loudly, faltering when he realized he had no idea what to say. "I… don't know what to say. I'm so sorry that this happened." His words sounded feeble even to his own ears. "I…"

"Why are we even listening to this kid, huh?" an angry voice called out – a human wearing leather armour stained grey with ash. "He has no idea what he's doing. Why's he even in charge?"

His words were met with murmurs of agreement.

"I'm…" Antimony tried to form the words to explain, but his pathetic attempt was quickly drowned out. Complaints and grumbles bubbled up like deadly lava, the crowd growing angry.

"I've said from the beginning this was all a stupid idea," a dwarf near the front proclaimed to those around him, just loud enough for Antimony to hear. "It's only because his mother's on the high council that we've had to come here. Well, look what a mess he's made! He should never have been put in charge. He's weird, always has been. The kid's not even smart enough to work out he's not a real dwarf. This whole palace malarkey is just another one of his fantasies. Maybe the council will see sense now."

Not a real dwarf? What did he mean?

"Bronze! How dare you say such things! I would have thought better of you," retorted Ma angrily. "The fact that Antimony is my son has nothing to do with this."

"You're right, Opal. It has nothing at all to do with it. He isn't even your son. Even a cave crab could see that. He's a human. We've all known it for years, but for some reason you ignore the fact, and he's too thick to understand. And now you've put him in charge of this crackpot scheme and it's all gone wrong. Maybe if you hadn't mollycoddled him so much–"

"Bronze! I am a member of the high–"

"I was quite happy in Val-Chasar, thank you very much. I didn't ask to be brought to this stupid ruin and get attacked."

Shouting broke out all over the place again. A few voices were raised in defence of Antimony and the project. Most shouted or complained about how stupid the whole thing was, and how all they wanted was to go home, and that Antimony should never have been in charge in the first place.

The human soldier who had started the grumbling shoved a nearby dwarf. A tussle broke out and others joined in.

The chaos washed over Antimony like background noise, disconnected from reality. His brain was replaying a thousand half-heard comments, funny looks, and awkward moments. Beyond the memories, the same words went round and round in his head: *He isn't even your son... He's a human... He's too thick to understand.* He had seen the panic and horror on Ma's face as she turned to look at him. And shame. She was ashamed of him. Her stupid son. No, not even her son. Just some human who had thought himself a dwarf!

Everything he thought he knew about himself crumbled in the wake of this revelation. Every childhood memory was changed in the light of this simple but terrible truth. In just a single moment, he understood why he had always been so much taller than the other dwarves; why he didn't have a beard; why he couldn't do the things other dwarves were good at.

He wasn't a dwarf. That was why.

Ma had known all along. She had thought him too slow to realize. She had been right.

It was as if someone had reached in and pulled out his very sense of self. Betrayed and more alone than he had thought possible, he stared at the woman he had always believed to be his mother and his world fell apart around him. She wasn't his mother. With that simple truth gone he didn't know who she was. He didn't know who *he* was.

Too many thoughts battled inside his head. Too many memories replaying and rewritten. Too many emotions swirling around in the tornado of his heart. Too much noise. Too much shouting. Why couldn't everyone stop shouting?

Without a word, Antimony turned and climbed down from his platform. The too-muchness was turning to numbness within him. He walked quickly across the ash and hot embers of the destroyed camp toward the gap in the wall, away from everything. He needed to be alone. He needed to escape this. All of this. He wished he could escape his own head.

Nobody wanted him there. He was different: not a dwarf, not a human, not wanted.

"Antimony!" a voice called across the burned camp, a voice hoarse with panic and choking back the tears. Once he would have called it Ma's voice, but he couldn't any more. She wasn't his ma.

"Antimony, my son. Come back!"

He didn't look back.

He walked faster.

The numbness solidified into an overwhelming sensation that went deeper than thoughts or words. It crushed his heart. Tears streamed down his face.

"Antimony!" The cry echoed inside the low palace wall, clear and piercing over the cacophony of the angry crowd and his own inner turmoil.

He ran.

He didn't know where he was running to, or why, but Antimony ran faster than he had ever run before. Down the palace hill and into the dark forest.

He took no notice of tree roots, bumps, bushes or rabbit holes. Though he stumbled, he kept running.

Low branches slapped his face. They clawed at his body, wanting to drag him back, but he kept going. In the deep, dark forest, the palace disappeared. The dense silence was broken only by the crashing of his own frenzied dash through the ancient trees.

He tripped. For a moment he flew, weightless in the air. The next moment he was sprawled in the leaf mulch, teeth-jarring pain shuddering through his body. The physical hurt did not compare with the wrenching agony he felt inside.

He lay as he had fallen, sprawled in the detritus of the forest floor. He tasted leaf mould. It was cold under his fingernails.

Wracking sobs shook his body.

Everything he had known, everything he had believed, was based on a lie. If he wasn't who he thought he was, then how could anything else be true?

He lay in the muck in his whirlpool of emotions for a long time. Eventually, the shaking sobs subsided. Numbness settled over him once more. Tears continued to stream, however, running down his cheeks and nose. They dripped onto the forest floor, creating a musky damp pool of muck.

He lay still, unable to get up. He couldn't move. He didn't want to. What was the point?

The sounds of the forest, drowned out or scared off by his uncontrolled sprint, slowly returned. Hesitantly, the hoots of owls, the rush of the wind in the trees and the rustling of small animals reasserted themselves. Antimony's world was shattered, yet the rest of the world continued as if it didn't care.

It wasn't fair.

What he would have given to be an owl or a field mouse or a tree; to be unconcerned and untouched by such pain.

Amid the natural noises of the wood he heard another sound. It was distant but approaching. It was the voice of a man singing, and as the voice drew nearer the words became distinct.

> *"Here in the Deepwood he called to me,*
> *Brother wolf, so regal and strong.*
> *I wanted to know how he could be free*
> *To sing in the moonlight his beautiful song.*
> *'Brother,' he told me, 'this is for you.*
> *Do not let bother weigh down on you.*
> *Run in the moonlight, sing to the moon,*
> *For here in the Deepwood there's space just for you.'"*

Antimony continued to lie where he had fallen. Nobody would see him in the dark. He barely spared a thought for the voice. It washed over him, oblivious to his numbness.

> *"Here in the Deepwood she came to me,*
> *Sister doe, so graceful and fleet.*
> *I wanted to know how she could be free*
> *To dance through the forest, on unburdened feet.*
> *'Sister,' she told me, 'this is for you.*
> *Do not run from things; only run to.*
> *Worry may follow, heartache may too,*
> *But here in the Deepwood there's space just for you.'"*

Slowly the voice penetrated Antimony's mind, just enough to cause a niggle of annoyance, distracting him from his self-pity. Who would be wandering through the woods so late at night, and singing?

> *"Then in the Deepwood, she spoke to me,*
> *'Wandering stranger, so lonely and low,*
> *You wanted to know how you could be free*
> *From trouble and heartache and sadness and woe.'*
> *'Friend,' said the Deepwood, 'this is for you.*
> *Life will have sorrow, but joys will come too.*
> *Never lose all hope, know this is true:*
> *Each dawn in the Deepwood you can hope anew.'"*

The voice was close now. As the song ended, the footsteps stopped too. Antimony heard a contented sigh as the singer sat down. Then there was nothing more than the living silence of the forest. In the distance, Antimony heard the faint, mournful howl of a wolf.

Time passed. He wasn't sure how much. The numbness had made time of no consequence.

After a fair while, however, Antimony found that his curiosity had grown stronger than the numbness.

Carefully, not wanting to make a sound, he lifted his head. Blinking dislodged a leaf that had stuck to his face. He squinted through the darkness in the direction from which the singing had come.

Close by was a small glade, lit by pale moonlight. Through a gap in the trees, Antimony could see stars glittering in the sky, a rare sight in Presadia nowadays. A man gazed up at the sky with an air of contentment about him. He looked as natural in the woods as the log he sat on. Antimony wondered if he was one of the human refugees. Or maybe he was one of the Usurper's men. No matter, he would surely leave soon.

Antimony lay his head back down on the ground. Although it was no longer all-consuming, the numbness was still there, and he was thankful for it. It was a dam holding back the flood of emotions, questions, and doubts that he didn't want to deal with. Yet, slowly the pain was beginning to trickle through.

The forest continued to breathe around him. Leaves rustled. The wind sighed. A nocturnal animal poked its way through the dead leaves.

The song echoed in his mind. The forest no longer seemed unfeeling. Instead, it appeared to welcome and embrace him without judgment or opinion. Here in the Deepwood Antimony could just be.

He might have dozed for a time – it was hard to tell. When eventually he lifted his head, his neck was stiff and he felt cold. He rolled onto his side and slowly sat up.

The man was still sitting on the log, not far away. He had been so still and quiet that Antimony had forgotten about him.

The man had his back to Antimony. Perhaps he had fallen asleep. Could he sneak away without alerting him?

He was just about to try when a voice made him jump.

"Well met, Antimony," said the man, without turning around.

22

THE MOONLIGHT WANDERER

Opal ran after Antimony, but his longer legs quickly outpaced hers. Fear made her shaky: the fear of losing her son; the fear of what she had done in keeping the truth from him.

She should have told him. She should have told him years ago. There had just never seemed to be the right moment. She had never been able to find the right words. It didn't matter to Opal that Antimony wasn't a dwarf. He was her son and she loved him more than anything in the world. She would willingly have died for him. Since the night Copper had first found him, Antimony had been the centre of her universe. The knowledge that she had ruined it all was like a heavy stone in the pit of her stomach.

The fact she had not given birth to him herself made him an even more precious gift. She had never thought she would have a child of her own, but then Antimony had been given to them. She hadn't ever thought of him as adopted; he had always simply been her son.

Shame mingled with fear. She hadn't told him, because deep down she had been afraid to. Afraid that by admitting the truth she might lose him; that he would no longer see her as his mother; that the perfect world she had created would crumble. She loved him so much that the thought of him taking back that love was like someone wrenching the very life out of her.

More than anything, she hadn't wanted to hurt him. But now she was afraid that she had hurt him even more.

She stumbled to the edge of the trees, calling frantically.

"Antimony! Antimony, come back! Please! Come back! I'm so sorry. Antimony!"

The silent forest loomed over her in disapproval.

Antimony – her only son – was gone.

Before him was the mysterious craftsman. The stranger from the ruins. The one who had fixed the mirror. Antimony was so taken aback that he forgot about his emotional turmoil for a moment.

"What brings you to the Deepwood this night?" the man asked, as if continuing a conversation with a friend he had bumped into in the street. He was still gazing up at the stars, his back to Antimony.

"How did you know I was here? Who are you, and why do you keep showing up?"

"So many questions. But I suppose I haven't answered many of them yet. In answer to your first question, I have been keeping a close watch on you. What you have been doing here is an excellent thing. As for the other questions, do you really not know who I am?"

"I'm not sure. At least..." Antimony cleared his throat, sure his hunch was going to sound silly. "Are you... Are you the king?"

The man swivelled to face him. "What makes you say that? I thought everyone knew the king was long gone."

Antimony's face grew hot. "It's just that... you seem to come and go as you like. You appear and disappear. I don't know how you do it, but I think it's something to do with the mirror. Khoree the dragon said the king was alive. She talked about how the mirrors were made by the king, and that he used them to move around. What you did with the mirror in my room…" He frowned, remembering. "*And* you knew my name before I ever told you, and – oh, I don't know. I just sort of… know. It's hard to explain. But it's not just in my head. I know it down here too." Antimony put his hand on his stomach, still feeling foolish. He was probably wrong. After all, why would the king care about following around someone as unimportant as he was?

"Ah, Khoree," said the man with a smile. "My old friend. How I look forward to meeting her again." He gave Antimony an appraising look. "You have a very quick and unique mind."

Antimony snorted. The man – the king – raised his eyebrow.

"I hate my mind," Antimony burst out. "It never stops plaguing me. It wastes time on stupid things."

"No one else in Presadia could do what you have done here, or so quickly."

"What? Make a huge mess?"

"The world is a mess, Antimony. It's what we choose to do about it that counts."

"What about when it's me that's the mess?"

"The same is true. Come and sit here with me. It's a beautiful night. We both know how rare that is in Presadia lately. The coming days will be worse than anything that has happened before."

Antimony sat down awkwardly beside the man, sensing the warmth of his body in the cool night air.

"Did you not learn anything from the mirror, Antimony?"

"What do you mean?"

"Remember its brokenness? For a time, you were ready to give up on it, to think it worthless and beyond hope. It takes perseverance and effort not to give up. Walking away is often the easiest thing to do, but mending something that is broken is always worth it. You think things are a mess, and perhaps they are. Your people are more fragile than any mirror. There are old divisions and breaks that run deep. Mending them never was going to be easy."

"It's not just that. I can't do it. I'm not the right person to be doing this. I never wanted to."

"We often have to do things we'd rather not."

"No one understands why we're building this stupid palace! Even I don't get it."

"And yet you have poured so much into it already. You must believe it to be the right thing."

"I did." Antimony hesitated. "I do still. But I'm not the right person to do it. No one wants me here."

"I don't believe that."

"It's true. You didn't hear what they all said. I'm a terrible leader. The dwarves don't want me, because I'm... I'm not a real dwarf. The humans don't want me, because I'm not a proper human. Even my parents – my real parents - didn't want me."

"Other people won't always give you what you need. They'll sometimes say nasty things, let you down or abandon you. But that's not who you are. And anyway, your parents *did* want you. They wanted you more than you can imagine."

"Then why didn't they keep me? Where are they? How did I end up in Val-Chasar?"

"All good questions. But I wasn't talking about those parents. I was talking about the parents who raised you and loved you as their own; who gave up many things to care for you, and who have always wanted the best for you."

Antimony sulked in silence for a moment. "I still don't belong though."

"What does belonging mean? If belonging is being the same as everyone else, then none of us belongs. Our uniqueness makes us who we are. Only you can be you, here or in Val-Chasar, or wherever you go. But I don't for a minute believe you don't belong,

Antimony. You have a mother who loves you dearly. I know it hurts to think of parents you have never known, but don't let that stop you from loving the parents you have had. Your family may not be the same as other families, but you do belong. Your parents chose you, Antimony, just as I chose you for this quest. We didn't have to. We chose you because we wanted you."

"You didn't choose me. I found *you*. And the ruins."

"Did you?"

Antimony didn't answer.

For a while, they sat in silence. The king had a comforting presence that reminded Antimony of his own father. That thought made him pause. Copper *had* been his father. And Opal *was* his mother. Yes, someone else might have given birth to him, but that didn't mean his parents weren't his parents.

Tears welled in his eyes once more. "I don't know who I am any more," he whispered.

The king placed his arm around Antimony's shoulder, giving it a gentle squeeze. Again, it reminded Antimony of the way his father had hugged him when he was small. There was security and strength in the touch.

"You are very special, and you are more valuable than the most precious silver or gold. To your ma, yes, but to many, many others too. To the whole of Presadia, in fact. There is only one of you – never forget that. And besides, even if no one else appreciated your value, Antimony, I would! I'm your king, and I wouldn't want a Presadia without you. Just as your parents made you part of their family, so I've chosen you too, for my kingdom."

The words seemed to trickle their way into Antimony's heart. Questions still remained – so many questions – but in the meantime he felt... safe. There was something about the man beside him that made Antimony believe what he said was true. He was still uncertain, still not sure he could go back to the palace and face everyone again, but the king's words and his comforting presence had given him strength.

"The world is growing darker and things will become more desperate," said the king. "But I have not given up on this kingdom. It may be a broken, diseased mess, but I remember it as it used to be. It's worth restoring, Antimony. The palace is more than a building. It stands for my rule over Presadia. That's why some will want to prevent it being rebuilt."

The king stood up. Dark clouds were rolling in to hide the stars once more. He turned to Antimony, his face earnest.

"Antimony, rebuild my palace. Work even harder and even faster to restore it so that you can defend it against the evil forces who challenge my rule. Time is running out. The Usurper will be back. Defend my kingdom against him. And welcome any who follow me.

"It will be hard – I can't deny that. But I will honour anyone who sacrifices themselves for me. Now, Antimony, will you pledge yourself to me?"

"No one will listen to me! Lots of them don't even believe you're still alive. But if you came with me and told them–"

"They will see me soon enough. For now, they're in your care, Antimony. I have other business to be about, but I know you can do this." He cocked his head, almost playfully. "If they doubt you, perhaps this will convince them. Something is about to happen that has not happened for a very long time. In the midst of the darkness there will be one who brings light and warmth and colour. From death and destruction will rise beauty and life.

"When it happens, tell everyone that it's a sign. There is hope in Presadia's despair. Anyone who follows me when I really don't look as though I am worth following will be greatly honoured when I rule this land once more." He winked at Antimony. "I'm hoping that won't be long now. So," his expression became serious again, "will you pledge yourself to me, Antimony?"

There was a long pause.

"I will," said Antimony.

The king smiled. "Then kneel, for today I make you a knight of Presadia. I have no dukedom or lavish gift to give you; only this."

From his coat he pulled out a small necklace. At the end was a single, uncut, mirrored jewel. *Majis-glatheras*. It glittered with different colours, and flickering pictures too small and fleeting for Antimony to take in.

"I have no high honour to bestow, but if you give me your word to serve me, I will give you my word that you will always have a place in my kingdom, and I will never forget your service or take it for granted.

"Serving me won't be easy. In the days to come, it may well bring down trouble on your head. It may demand even your life. But remember, I stand by those who stand by me."

Antimony's heart pounded, yet in spite of his trepidation, there was a certainty and a rightness he had never felt before. He kneeled, and the king placed his hand on his head.

"Antimony, I choose you to be my knight; a representative of my rule and reign in Presadia. Will you stand for me in word and action? Will you defend the defenceless, lift up the downtrodden and speak up for those who have no voice? Will you free the oppressed and welcome in the lonely? Will you give of yourself to serve me and the people of Presadia? Will you be my herald in every forgotten corner of my kingdom? Will you choose me above all, over any other lord and king?"

"Yes," said Antimony. "I will."

The king placed the necklace over Antimony's head.

"Arise then, Antimony, Knight of Presadia."

23

LIGHT AND COLOUR

Hazel Crumpetbottom rubbed her aching back. A storm was coming – she could feel it in her bones. It would be a terrible one; she just knew it.

She hobbled over to her hearth and stoked the burning coals that were doing their best to drive back the damp cold of her cottage. She lifted the bucket of water onto the hook above the fire. In her youth, she had always washed in cold water, but now she was older she found the warmth helped her aching joints.

She turned to get some herbs for the washing water, and stopped.

The ripples in the water caught the light. For an instant she had seen a flash of colour and movement.

Silly old woman, she chided herself.

She was becoming just as ridiculous as the villagers. All day long people had been coming to tell her their dreams and visions: a reflection in the teapot, a vision in a metal spoon, even an image on the point of a needle. Wiggleswandians were a superstitious bunch. Once one person thought they had seen a vision, everyone else jumped on the apple cart. Only a month ago she'd had half the village banging on her door because they had seen a black demon stalking through the village, stealing their food. It had been nothing more than the baker's cat!

She chose one of her little boxes of gathered ingredients and added a pinch of dried lavender and wiggle petals to the water. As the leaves settled on the water the surface bloomed into vivid colour.

Hazel Crumpetbottom stared open-mouthed at the vision in her bucket.

By the time Antimony had made his way back to the construction site, the first light of morning was trying to break on the horizon. But the sun was hidden behind the dark, brooding clouds that had closed heavily over the half-burned camp, and the gloom lifted only slightly in the east, as if the sky were trying to match Antimony's own sombre mood.

The king had led him back to the edge of the forest. Antimony had looked up at the palace hill, considering what was before him. When he turned back, the king had vanished.

There was a lone figure sitting on the hill, looking out over the forest. Ma.

Tears had streaked pale stripes through the grimy dust on her face. Her shoulders sagged; her hair and beard were a dishevelled mess. No longer the blazing warrior who had come leaping through the magic portal, this was a distraught mother. But Antimony knew that she was stronger and more determined than the mightiest soldier.

And yet, in that moment, she looked broken. Not broken by the angry crowd, or by the blazing fires of the previous night, or by the enormity of the mission to restore the palace. No, she had been broken by Antimony running away from her.

He hurried toward her. He was still a good distance away when she saw him. There was none of the dignity of a high council member as she ran to him, arms wide open, tears streaming down her dirty cheeks.

"Antimony! Oh, Antimony! You've come back. I'm sorry. I should have told you years ago. Thank goodness you've come back!"

Antimony's eyes filled with tears too. How he had any left in him he didn't know. He broke into a run before falling to his knees to throw his arms around her.

"Antimony, my son, my love. I'm so, so sorry."

"No, Ma. I'm sorry. I had to… I just needed to think for a while."

"I should have told you, but the moment never seemed to be right. At first I didn't realize that you… b-but you just kept growing. It didn't matter to us. We loved you so much. *I* love you so much."

"I love you too, Ma."

He buried his face in her soft beard, smelling the smoke from the fires mixed with her own familiar smell. There were a thousand questions whizzing around his head, but in that moment the hug was enough.

"Oh, Antimony, can you ever forgive me?"

He drew back and smiled into her tear-streaked face. "Of course, Ma."

"You were our gift. Our precious gift. We had wanted a baby for so long. We had almost given up hope. But then we found you, all alone, deep underground in a section of the mines no one had used for a long time. I've no idea how you got there or where you came from. It seemed too magical to be real.

"I loved you from the very first moment I saw you. Nobody knew about where you had come from. It seemed to us we were meant to find you. You were meant to be ours. I can't explain it. I wanted to, a thousand times, but I could never find the right words."

"So you don't know where I came from or who my parents – my other parents – are?"

She shook her head.

"Ma, I want to know everything you know. But not now – later on. You see, I just met…" Antimony hesitated. He knew that what he was about to say was going to sound insane.

"Ma, I just met the king. The real king. There's too much to explain right now, but he found me in the forest. He's the man from the ruins, remember? The man who fixed the mirror. He knows everything about me. He wants us to keep going and finish the palace. I know it sounds crazy, but it's true."

There was confusion on Ma's face. She looked at him hard, as if seeking out the truth of what he had said. "The king? The *real* king, here in the forest?"

"Yes. He's alive, Ma! He said things are going to get bad, but we need to keep going. I have to go back and gather the people."

"Most of the people are getting ready to leave. They're angry and frightened after the raid. The situation got even more heated when you left. In the end I had to let the dwarves who came with me go back to Val-Chasar. Most of the humans are leaving as well."

"They can't! Not now. The king said we have to complete the palace. We need to go faster and work even harder. They can't go."

"It's too late. They're already leaving."

"We have to convince them, Ma."

Seeing his resolve, she nodded. "We can try. We'd better go quickly. They were intending to head back to the portal at daybreak, and despite these horrible clouds, I think it's dawn already."

Together they hurried up the slope toward the palace entrance. The ground had been churned up by the workers, and the raiders' horses, making it slippery and hard going.

At the top, Antimony looked between the half-built walls and across the large, desecrated expanse of burned camp. At the edge of the fire-scorched earth, workers were loading the remaining supplies into hastily fashioned packs and sledges. Nearby, a large group of elves stood in a huddle; as many as a hundred of them, Antimony guessed, his mind already working on a more accurate count.

Ma saw them too. "Tommarind's messengers returned from the Silverwood with reinforcements only an hour or so ago," she said.

The elves appeared to be discussing what to do. Antimony felt a pang of regret. If only they had arrived a few hours earlier, the scores of longbows would have held back the small raiding party with no trouble.

There was a clear division between the groups in the camp. Dwarves, elves, and humans kept to themselves. A fourth group, containing only a handful of people, including Salt, Zil, and a smattering of humans and dwarves, sat to one side, watching in frustrated silence.

Antimony hurried across the aftermath of the battle, Ma at his side, walking over the remains of half-burned tools, charred wood, and trampled possessions. Ash swirled in small eddies like grey snow as a growing wind whipped around the circular wall.

"Stop!" Antimony called. "Don't leave. You have to stay and help."

Some of the people turned to look at him. He heard resentful grumbles, but none of the angry shouts and insults of the previous night. Others ignored him and carried on with their preparations, slinging bags onto shoulders or tying scavenged supplies to the sledges.

"Please listen. Leaving now would be a mistake."

"Listen, kid." It was the man in armour from the night before. "The only mistake we've made is listening to you for this long. If you have something to say, you should have said it last night. We're going back to Val-Chasar, and then on to make our own way in the world."

"That's right," a surly dwarf added, annoyed at a human speaking for them all. "We're going back too. And don't you go changing your mind, Opal. You've already said we can."

"I did, Bronze, but hear Antimony out. If you still want to leave then, I won't stop you."

There was a lump in Antimony's throat that made it hard to speak. He reached up to grasp the necklace the king had given him, pulling it over his head so that he could hold it in his hand. Somehow, the cool, jagged crystal gave him strength and helped him to form the words he needed.

"I know how you all feel. I'm sorry about what happened last night. I understand why you want to give up. I wanted to give up too. To have those creatures ruin all our hard work and worrying that they might come back makes keeping going sound stupid. But if we stop now, not only has the Usurper won, but we have lost. And we will have lost more than just a camp and these ruins. We will have lost the symbol of the king's rule, here in Presadia. We will have lost hope that good may yet return.

"This is the king's palace. Presadia is his kingdom. We must stand up and defend him if we want to help restore Presadia and make it better again. I know it's just half-built walls and ash at the moment. I know it looks broken and beyond repair. But out of ashes and brokenness can come beauty. This place will show that the king still rules Presadia."

Antimony felt pleased with his speech until he looked at the faces before him. They were unimpressed and doubtful.

"Fancy words, boy," the human soldier scoffed, "but the king *doesn't* reign in Presadia. He hasn't been around for hundreds of years. The king is dead; dead or given up on us. I don't know why you're so obsessed."

"He does!" insisted Anthony. "He does still reign. He *is* alive."

The people shook their heads and turned back to their preparations. With a dismissive wave of his hand the outspoken man led the group of humans toward the palace exit.

"It's true!" There was a note of desperation in Antimony's voice now. "I was with him only minutes ago. He told me we need to keep going."

"Bah!" Bronze replied. He turned and signalled to the dwarf group to follow him.

"Please, stay!"

Everyone ignored him. It was just as Antimony had feared. They wouldn't listen. He had told the king they wouldn't. He remembered the king's promise that there would be a sign and looked around, hoping for something to happen, but nothing did.

He saw only heavy storm clouds and the muddy greyness of the ash-covered camp.

Then Antimony's hand thrummed. Opening his clenched fist, he stared in amazement at the shard of king's glass. Dazzling rainbows of colour burst out onto the burned ground around him. Within its radiance, hints of visions and pictures flashed, too numerous to take in. Antimony held out his hand, squinting against the brilliance. It was like staring into Sparks' cage when she was at her brightest.

Murmurs of astonishment and wonder rose up from the assembled workers. Antimony held the crystal high, feeling it grow warm in his hand.

He thought back to the king's words, each one recalled perfectly, as if they echoed out from the shining crystal.

In the midst of the darkness there will be one who brings light and warmth and colour.

His voice carried around the amphitheatre of the half-finished wall. "There is hope in Presadia's despair."

The stone grew hotter.

"I am a knight of Presadia and a herald of the king – the true king of Presadia. He will return."

Antimony tore his eyes from the dazzling jewel in his hand to look at the workers around him. They all gaped at him, their mouths open wide in awe at this outlandish display of magic.

"Please help me. Help me rebuild the palace. Help me restore this symbol of the king's rule in Presadia. Help me defend it from any who seek to stop him."

Zil was the first to step forward, still mesmerized by the stone, her wide eyes reflecting the dazzling light. "I'll help," she said.

Ma was next. "Till my dying breath!"

"Great Potash's beard. How could I do anything else?" said Salt.

No one else stepped forward. The stone held them spellbound, but there was still too much uncertainty about Antimony's grand claims.

The stone grew hotter still. It was burning his hand, too hot to hold. The light was now so intense they could no longer look at it, no matter how much they squinted.

"Ouch!"

Antimony snatched back his burned hand, letting the gem fall to the floor. Flickers of light sparkled as it hit the ground. A ripple pulsed through the ash, crackling with tiny bolts of white-hot lightning. It spread outwards toward the walls, and as it neared the open gateway, a sharp crack echoed around the palace compound.

A lump in the ash shifted ominously.

24

FROM THE ASHES

The fire had done its work. Sparks had absorbed it, drawn it into herself, letting it change her and feed her. The untameable fire had given her its power. Around her the ash had hardened into a secure cocoon. Within it she had shed her outer layer.

She wriggled, half surprised, yet deep down anticipating the strange sensation of her new form.

She wriggled again, scratching herself against the solid ash.

She was frustrated at her lack of coordination. And weak. She craved more power, more energy, to finish the process; to break free from the cocoon; to live as she was meant to live.

In the meantime, she settled herself, allowing her new muscles to relax. Thoughts and memories, clearer and more distinct than she had ever experienced, raced through her mind. Strange memories of her time in her old form, dull and unthinking, aware of so little.

Hmmmmmm.

There was someone… The kind one. A name…

An...

Her memory was interrupted.

Energy shivered through her body. Her mind cleared further. How foggy and dim-witted it had been until then! Finally, her thoughts were clear and sharp.

The awakening brought a swell of elation. Suddenly she understood what each new muscle was for. Heaving herself up, she felt the ash cocoon flex against her. The wave of energy had filled her with strength. Spreading her new wings, she leapt, shattering the cocoon and bathing her in a cloud of ash dust.

Sparks' senses bloomed. Her new eyes took in the universe of sights and colours. Her ears gathered up the echoed symphony of sounds belonging to the world beyond a lantern. She smelled the vivid and powerful scent trails and was instantly intoxicated by the secrets within them. Among them was one that seemed… familiar. She wasn't sure how, since she had never been able to smell before, but the instinct was strong.

The kind one, she thought, clawing at the distant memory, trying to draw out information she had been too dull to understand at the time.

Antimony.

There was an explosion of ash and still-smouldering embers as something burst out of the burned mess. Ruby red and glittering, it launched itself upwards over the grey field of ash. Elegant wings, almost transparent, stretched wide on either side.

Gasps of fear and astonishment rose up from the assembled crowd. Antimony watched in wonder as a small dragon emerged from the explosion and took its first flight. It wasn't a particularly long flight. In fact, Antimony had the distinct feeling that the dragon wasn't entirely sure how to fly.

After a strange twisting manoeuvre, the creature glided toward the crowd, landing only paces away. The workers shied away in alarm. Lifting its muzzle, the young dragon gave a half-cough, half-roar. A small bubble of flame erupted from the toothless mouth.

The king's words echoed in Antimony's mind.

Something is about to happen that has not happened for a very long time. In the midst of the darkness there will be one who brings light and warmth and colour. From death and destruction will rise beauty and life.

"Mmmmmm," said the dragon in a croaky voice, unused to forming sounds. It lingered on each syllable, as if enjoying the new sensation. "An-tim-ony."

The dragon waddled toward him, lifting its muzzle to sniff curiously at his filthy clothes. The scaled nose was warm as it brushed over him with a fondness that took Antimony by surprise. Its breath was musty, like the air from a disused cavern.

Something about this creature was familiar.

It rubbed its head against his hand before stretching its head to expose a long, pale neck. He waited, wondering what he was supposed to do. Nervously, he reached out his hand and ran it along the dragon's neck. The scales were a milky orange on the underside, soft and slightly gummy, not hard and polished like Khoree's had been. The baby dragon was spindly. Instead of Khoree's rippling muscles and toughened wings, its skin was stretched over delicate, slender bones. This dragon was a fraction of Khoree's size, slightly shorter than Antimony himself. It was unmistakably a dragon, however.

The small dragon pressed harder against his hand. He took the hint, scratching and tickling its long neck. As he did, the creature shivered with pleasure, wriggling in a way that reminded him of…

"Sparks?" he said, doubtfully.

The dragon looked at him. "Mmmmmmmmm. An-tim-ony."

How? Antimony stared. What under earth could have happened to his magma-worm to turn her into this?

The workers were mumbling and chattering among themselves, awed silence giving way to an excited hubbub.

"It's a sign!" said one.

"I don't believe it!" said another.

The workers shuffled closer to Antimony and Sparks, leaving their sledges and bags behind, united in marvelling at the spectacle.

Tommarind walked toward Antimony and laid his hand flat on the ashy ground.

"Antimony, I ask your forgiveness."

"Why?"

"I doubted your story. But this? A new dragon has not appeared since the king reigned, and even in those days such an event was incredibly rare. For elves, humans, dwarves – and now dragons – to be gathered together, here of all places… I don't believe this can be mere chance. This has to be the king's work.

"It was the king who first united the four great races. Today, I see that they can be reunited again. I don't pretend to understand, but this I know: you are a trustworthy man to follow. We will help you rebuild. We will do whatever we can to heal the Great Silvers and restore the keep."

"Thank you, Tommarind," said Antimony, relieved.

"My!" Salt exclaimed. "First a long-lost palace, then this Usurper fellow, and now a new dragon. We really have stumbled into the time of legends. I think Khoree the dragon was correct. I think you, my dear boy, are correct. The king *is* alive. By my beard! He deserves a proper palace, and a throne room too."

"Antimony," said Ma, "I have to return to Val-Chasar. I must update the high council. They'll never believe all that's happened."

Sparks was still nuzzling him as Zil stepped forward. Gently she stroked the dragon's head. Sparks turned to her, cocking her reptilian head to examine the young woman.

"She's so beautiful!" Zil said. "She looks like fire. Did you say her name is Sparks?"

"I think it must be Sparks. But I don't know how this happened.

I don't remember reading anything about magma-worms turning into dragons. Perhaps that's how it always happens."

"Just like you to be talking about dusty books when you have a real-life dragon in front of you," Zil laughed. "Hello, Sparks. My name is Zil."

"Mmmmmm... Zzzzil," the dragon repeated, savouring the sound. "Zil."

"She said my name! I didn't know dragons could speak."

"I'll tell you all about Khoree some time," Antimony said.

"I'd love that." The excitement on her face was genuine. "But not right now. We've got too much to do. We need to get back to work as fast as possible. We must get this palace into a more defendable state in case that swine Wolf-ear, or this Usurper fellow, shows up."

"But I thought everyone was planning on leaving."

"After that display?" Zil grinned at him. "Oi! Listen up, everyone. Is there anyone still too thick-headed to see that what's happening here is special? I know what Antimony's told us sounds strange, but a real-life dragon appearing is even stranger. Even if the king isn't here, why should we let that stinker, the Usurper, trample all over us? I believe Antimony. I believe the king is alive. But even if you don't, do you really think you can find anything more exciting to do than this? If you wanna go, then go. But if you think that we're doing something worthwhile, then I say we get back to work."

Antimony stared at her in admiration. Her courage was contagious.

And it seemed to be just what the workers needed to rouse them from their dazed state. People were nodding and voicing their agreement.

"Right then," Zil continued, "let's get back to work. And keep something nearby to defend yourself with, just in case those nasty horsemen decide to come back."

Just like that, it all seemed to be decided. With excited chattering and wide-eyed glances at Sparks, the people hurried away to get on with their work.

25

THE GATHERING STORM

Far to the east of Presadia's borders, in a place where dwarves, elves, and humans had never set foot, Karagnoord bent his ancient neck to drink from the icy pool. As his muzzle broke the still water, a hiss of steam erupted.

Ripples spread out, distorting his reflection. His yellow-green scales and bone-white tusks disintegrated into a pattern of dappled colours.

He lapped the water, feeling its cooling balm against his warm tongue. His mind was blank. There was little to fill it any more. So many years had passed since he had come to live here alone.

He had thought about everything there was to think about – and thought it a thousand times. There was little point thinking it all over again; it would only make him angry, hot and bothered. Not thinking made his exile and solitude more bearable.

He watched the changing patterns on the water's surface. Green, yellow, the grey of the sky. The same patterns he saw every day, and yet always different and unique. Never identical but always predictable. Like morning and evening.

Green, yellow, grey.
Green, yellow, grey.
Green, yellow…
Red.

He raised his head abruptly and looked around to see what had disturbed the reflection. There was nothing but the barren grey mountains and moody sky.

The ripples settled, and red flowed over the surface of the water like spilled oil, then other colours formed a reflection; the reflection of another place.

Unusual, Karagnoord thought. *Very unusual.*

Magic and visions didn't disturb a dragon of his years. He had seen magic before, a thousand times. But not, he considered, in the hundreds of years since his long hermitage had begun.

Something was happening.

He turned back to the vision. There was a human boy – young man, perhaps. Karagnoord barely knew the difference. Humans lived for so short a time, it was a wonder they bothered to divide up their few years into childhood and adulthood.

It was as if the pool were held in the boy's upraised hand, and he was staring at Karagnoord in wonder. Could the human see him too?

The young human stood on a rock amid the blackened remains of a burned encampment. He was covered in ash and mud. Karagnoord felt he knew the place, though there was little to tell him where it was. Around the boy were elves, dwarves, and humans. How curious.

An echo of the distant past came to him, when such intermingling had been common. He leaned closer. Hot breath from his nostrils disturbed the water. The vision lurched. When it settled again, the viewpoint was different. He was watching the scene from low down on the ground, beside the rock on which the boy stood. A flash of fire, and in the distance a red shape erupted from the ash, twisted in the air, and glided toward the human. It landed on the ground, clumsy but triumphant, before arching its slender neck to trumpet into the sky, a tiny glob of flame shooting from its lips.

Could it be? A new dragon? Freshly transformed, by the looks of things. Karagnoord tilted his head in interest. There had been no new dragons for many generations. Not since that terrible business with the king of Presadia, when any dragon with good sense had fled the forsaken kingdom. And now? Why now? A new dragon was never insignificant.

If this vision were real – and Karagnoord had no reason to suspect otherwise – then something was happening in Presadia; something important that might change everything.

Karagnoord lifted his head and bellowed his own triumphant roar at the empty sky, to welcome his little sister. The vibrations rippled the pool and the vision vanished as quickly as it had appeared. The echoes were still bouncing between the empty mountaintops as Karagnoord took to the air and beat his great wings westward.

It was the fourth morning after Sparks' miraculous transformation.

The workers had thrown themselves into the project with an enthusiasm and vigour beyond anything Antimony could have hoped for. The wall was almost finished. Today they were working on the parapet, the little wall around the top to stop people falling over the edge.

The stone was bare, not white and gleaming as it had been in Antimony's vision, but it was still impressive to look at.

With the elven reinforcements, the healing and regrowth of the Great Silvers was almost complete. Even with so many, it had taken a full day to remove all signs of the black disease from the twelve trees. Then the truly astounding work had begun, the magic the people had wanted to see. With five or six elves at each stump they had whispered to the trees, urging them to grow. And grow they had, faster than Antimony had ever believed possible.

He had stared in amazement as the stumps lengthened and new shoots sprouted before his eyes. Sap oozed as the silky bark stretched upwards. Each passing minute saw the trees grow a hand's breadth taller, creaking and groaning as they inched their way higher. Under the elves' gentle direction, they turned as they grew, weaving themselves in the graceful twisting spiral Antimony recognized as the tower he had seen in his vision. The work clearly took a huge toll on the elves in terms of energy and effort, but seeing the trees healed and growing once more also filled them with joy.

Antimony marvelled at the pace of their work. Already there was a spacious room on the ground floor, as high as the palace wall, well over twice Antimony's height. Young branches had been directed inwards to create a spiral of beams over what would one day be the throne room.

Antimony was used to the simple materials of stone, metal, and sawn wood. Dwarves planned everything out, cut materials to size, and fitted them all together. With elves, building was more like sculpting, or choreographing an incredibly slow dance between the twelve trees. Before a dwarfish or human building was finished, it looked half done, but the keep the elves were constructing looked complete, even now. Antimony had to keep reminding himself that the tower was formed of trees. Unlike constructions of stone and metal, they were alive, evolving and changing. Even when the elves were done, the keep would continue to grow and mature. Who would have thought you could grow a building!

He turned from the remarkable keep and walked toward the gateway in the palace wall. A wooden palisade and a thick gate now filled the gap, while they worked out how to make the huge metal gate he had seen in his vision. They could have forged it in the great workshops of Val-Chasar, but getting it through the portal would have been impossible. Short of a dragon carrying it from Val-Chasar, Antimony was at a loss. It was a problem for another day.

The camp had been rebuilt. Wooden shelters had replaced the tents, leaning against the inside of the wall. One day, they would be replaced by permanent stone buildings.

Ma had taken word of the new dragon, and Antimony's meeting with the king, to the other members of the high council. They had decided to come through to see for themselves what all the fuss was about. Sparks had amazed them, and the stone pendant had helped convince some of them that the king really had been there, though Antimony knew some still doubted. Additional supplies and weapons were sent through from Val-Chasar, and permission was given to any dwarf who wanted to help to come through the portal and contribute to the building of the palace.

Antimony had been overwhelmed by the response. Hundreds more dwarves had flooded through the portal. Even one of the high council members stayed to help: Granite Greybeard, the miserable old dwarf who had criticized the scheme so vociferously at the beginning. The new contingent of dwarves had been joined by more refugees. Some had apparently turned up at Val-Chasar, chattering excitedly about strange visions of "the boy and the dragon". Antimony didn't know what to make of that, but welcomed anyone who wanted to help.

He was now responsible for hundreds of people, effectively a whole town. Alongside the main encampment on the hill, there was a second camp by the quarry. Here another palisade had been built, and the portal had become a gatehouse, guarded by a permanent garrison of dwarves defending the back door into Val-Chasar.

Both the palace mound and the quarry encampment were secured during the night-time hours. Each morning, however, seemed dimmer than the last. The days were growing as gloomy as the nights. Bubbling yellow-black clouds obscured the sky. Soon it would be dark enough in the daytime that they would need to journey outside into the black forest whatever time of day it was.

Breakfast had ended and a small queue was forming as people waited to head out to the quarry or back to Val-Chasar. Antimony looked up at the dark sky, trying to gauge the hour and whether he should order the gates to be opened.

There had been no more raids on the camp, though Antimony had received reports of enemy scouts among the trees. He had sent patrols to investigate, but the enemy always managed to slink away into the darkness of the forest.

He wondered if the Usurper and his troops had expected them to run away. Maybe they wouldn't try to take on such a large camp, now they were alert and ready to defend themselves. Antimony knew frustratingly little about his enemy. The elves had told him about a stronghold in the forest, but they had avoided going near it. Antimony had no way of knowing how many thugs were on their doorstep, but it would take a proper army to attack the palace mound now. Maybe the Usurper didn't have that kind of army, in spite of what the librarian had said about how he was gathering a vast force in order to conquer Presadia. Still, Antimony did not want to take any chances. He'd made that mistake before.

As each day grew darker, the yellow fog got thicker, forcing them to wrap cloths over their mouths and noses to filter out the poisonous air. Even so, the coughing became worse. Thunder rumbled in the distance and the air was sluggish and heavy, as if a mighty storm were brewing. But still it did not break. This morning felt different, though. Rather than the heavy dense air that usually accompanied the fog, a breeze was ruffling Antimony's hair. Antimony hoped it would clear the terrible mists, but at the moment it only seemed to be pulling more fog in its wake.

It wasn't only the weather that was feeding Antimony's anxiety. The forest had grown eerily quiet, as if the birds and animals had vanished. What had scared them away? What ominous thing was about to happen?

He heard a whistle from the top of the wall. It was Zil, standing with one of the guards and signalling for Antimony to join them. He made his way over to the rickety ladder.

He liked being up on the wall. It gave him an excellent view over the camp. In spite of his worries, he was filled with pride as he looked down on it. Not pride in himself, but for everything they had achieved together. Relationships between the races were mending as they worked side by side each day. The dwarves would lead people in jolly songs and chants. The humans, it turned out, were superb cooks, and they also had a talent for telling jokes that would have the camp in tears of laughter. The elves had taken to telling stories of the good king around the campfires at night. Despite their differences, they were a community.

Antimony had told his friends about his meetings with the king, although he had left out the most personal parts. The stories had spread and grown, as stories do, in the retelling. Antimony had even heard the ridiculous suggestion that the king had given him a suit of shining armour, and a sword taller than six dwarves standing on each other's shoulders!

"Morning, sleepyhead," said Zil.

"Morning," he replied, nodding a greeting to the guard. He didn't know her personally but recognized her as one of Zil's friends. It seemed to him that Zil was friends with everyone.

"I was just bringing Sav some breakfast and she said she thought she had spotted smoke."

"Smoke? Where?"

"Beggin' ya pardon, Master Antimony, but I don't know as it's smoke for sure. The mist is proper thick out there."

"It's not *Master* Antimony. Just Antimony. And it doesn't matter if you're not sure. Tell me where you think you saw it."

"All over. In the west there, but also over 'ere."

Antimony squinted. The patches of yellow fog were thicker and the tendrils of mist did look like smoke.

"Ma said about sending out a patrol this morning. I'll tell them to be extra careful."

"I like your ma," Zil said. "She doesn't take any nonsense. Hey!"

Zil jumped back as Sparks swooped in to land on the wall near Antimony. Her flying was improving every day. She was learning quickly, though her vocabulary was still very basic. She was clearly clever, though. She'd also put on muscle and weight. She ate almost continuously and spent most of her time each day hunting. Antimony wondered how she was able to find the Great Forest's elusive animals.

Antimony scratched under her chin. "Morning, Sparks," he said.

"Antimony," the dragon purred.

"She really is beautiful!" Zil marvelled.

Sparks turned to Zil and acknowledged the compliment by lowering her head so that Zil could scratch it. After a moment she shook herself and stepped up to the edge of the wall before launching herself into the air again.

"Sssssssky," she hissed as she beat her way upwards.

No one would be foolish enough to think she belonged to him. She might show Antimony affection, but she had a mind of her own. He had already seen flashes of temper that reminded him of Khoree. She went where she willed and was gone longer and longer each day. Antimony, Zil, and her friend Sav admired her shrinking form as she raced away.

"She's amazing. It's unfair that she likes you best," said Zil.

"I think she remembers me from when she was a magma-worm," explained Antimony. "Anyway, time is getting on and people are starting to queue up. I came over to open the gates."

"Oooh... Can I do it?" Zil asked excitedly.

"Be my guest." Antimony was getting used to her endless energy and passion. She appeared to be involved in everything in the camp and she clearly enjoyed bossing people around.

He jumped at the volume of her bellow.

"OPEN THE GATES!"

Down below, some of the queuing workers also looked up in surprise. A few scurried to lift the great bar that secured the gate. It swung open and the workers started passing through.

"I'm going to go and visit Salt in the quarry camp," Zil announced, turning toward the ladder. "I didn't see him yesterday."

Antimony noticed movement at the edge of the forest.

"Wait!" he called after her.

Zil turned back, and the workers nearest the gate stopped and looked up in alarm.

A line of dark figures emerged from the trees.

26

THE VISION CHASERS

Hazel Crumpetbottom had been nervous about leading her people into the Deepwood, though she would never have said that to them. They leaned on her as if she were one of the oldest trees in the forest. To them she was just as ancient and just as unmovable. If only they had known!

Everyone had heard stories about the Deepwood, or the Great Forest as some folk liked to call it. It was said that a dark presence lived in the forest. Few went into the Deepwood and even fewer returned. There were stories of terrible and hideous creatures prowling in there.

Hazel had little time for superstition, but there was a kernel of truth to most stories.

Her small flock had followed her hesitantly under the dark canopy and along the uneven, moss-covered flagstones of the old King's Road. It was barely visible to those who didn't know what to look for. Despite living on its border their entire lives, few had ventured further than a dozen paces into the forest. It simply wasn't safe.

Hazel Crumpetbottom knew that. But she also knew what the vision had told her. After the boy and the dragon, she had seen the King's Road, where it entered the primeval forest. She had known, with the gut sense that all wise women have, that they were supposed to go there. And so they had. Every last one of them. The entire village: thirty-one souls.

On the evening of the third day they stumbled upon a junction with a crumbling, weathered marker. Hazel didn't know whether they should go north or west. The vision hadn't shown her that.

Tired and unsure, they had just decided to make camp when they heard the sound of horses' hooves.

Quickly, the Wiggleswandians had scattered into the brush and darkness under the trees to watch, holding their breath as a column of darkly clad troops came along the path from the west and turned up the northern track. The column had been headed by horsemen and led by a blood-red elf. Hazel Crumpetbottom had heard that elves had tattooed heads rather than hair. This elf had only scarring. It looked as if he had burned off his tattoos.

The sight of the horsemen was enough to make Hazel Crumpetbottom believe demons rode among them. The riders had pieces of animal attached to their armour, and even to their bodies. Teeth, bones, skin, claws, and antlers, mutilated versions of the animals to which they had once belonged. Some wore wigs of hair with tusks and snouts; others had attached spikes of bone to their shaved heads. Some had sewn long claws onto their hands, and Hazel Crumpetbottom even saw a man who had replaced his own teeth with the sharp canines of a dog or wolf. Foam dribbled from his jaw as if he were a slavering animal.

Hazel averted her eyes to stop the bile that was rising within her. It was deeply unnatural and sickening.

After the horsemen came many people on foot. Rank after untidy rank. These soldiers weren't as heavily mutilated as the horsemen but were still adorned with the body parts of various animals. Their weapons and equipment were rusty and painted black. They looked poorly fed and sickly. There was no sign of warmth or friendship between them. Each looked mistrustful and shifty, like a convict waiting to be sentenced.

The Wiggleswandians had huddled, barely breathing, while the column passed by; endless dark figures like wraiths of the underworld.

Near the end of the column were long lines of prisoners tied together at wrist and ankle to prevent them running away. They were barefoot, their clothing scant and threadbare. Hazel Crumpetbottom spotted a face among the prisoners that made her blood freeze.

Young Elias, Gannapple's boy. The child who had gone missing only the week before. She raised a hand to stifle her gasp.

Antimony let out his breath. The group by the tree line appeared to be a cluster of human peasants. He counted quickly: thirty-one in total, ranging from babes in arms to a woman at the front who looked older than the forest itself. They didn't look like the Usurper's troops. More refugees from Val-Chasar, he decided with a frown. The portal encampment wasn't meant to open its gates until a messenger from the palace came with the prearranged password.

The group were running, casting fearful glances behind them at the trees, as if something pursued them. Parents carried children, and the old hobbled along with help from the young. The wizened old woman barked at the others to go faster.

"Come on, Zil," said Antimony. "Let's find out what's going on."

They slid down the ladder and squeezed their way past the huddle of people at the gate. A few dwarves and humans grabbed weapons and hurried out to stand alongside Antimony and Zil as they waited at the top of the hill.

"They come. The demon army. They come!" The old woman's words were shouted with a strength Antimony had not expected from such a frail body.

The guards nearest him muttered in an anxious buzz.

"Demon army?" Zil repeated back. She sounded almost excited. Antimony, on the other hand, felt a cold sweat break out on his neck.

"They are all around, in the trees. They come. They come!" the woman cried again.

The small group reached the bottom of the hill and started clambering up in desperation.

"Who are you?" Antimony asked.

"Good folk. Peaceful folk. We chase visions. Visions of this place and a dragon and…" Antimony found himself under the eagle-eyed examination of the woman. "Ah… and you. The boy on the rock. We've found you, thank the forest! But there is no time. The enemy gathers around us."

Even as she said the words, Antimony saw a shadow shift under the trees. The haze of yellow mist made it hard to see, but there was no doubt that there were many dark shapes moving around beneath the dense canopy.

"It's the Usurper!" Zil gasped.

"Raise the alarm," said Antimony, as calmly as possible.

Zil rushed back to the palace. A few moments later, Antimony heard the trumpeting blast of the warning signal. He had prepared them for this. Everyone should know what to do. There was shouting and the trample of feet as people raced to grab weapons and take up battle positions in their groups.

The shapes began to emerge from the trees. Black forms. Antimony's brain tried to count them, but there were so many and they seemed to dissolve in and out of the mist.

The panicked peasants were nearing the top of the hill. They looked harmless enough, but he didn't want to be fooled by some ploy of the Usurper.

"Who are you?" he asked again.

"I told you, we come in peace. We are from Wiggleswand, in the Deepwood borderlands. The visions led us here, but the enemy is close behind us. I feared we wouldn't make it through the night."

They reached the top of the hill, and Antimony's guards stepped forward with their weapons drawn, waiting for him to give the go-ahead. The old woman and her companions stopped, panting from their run up the hill.

"I'm Hazel Crumpetbottom, wise woman of Wiggleswand–"

"Hazel–"

"Crumpetbottom, yes. And you are the boy with the dragon. There's no time for pleasantries. An army of half-beasts waits below. We wish to join your fight against them."

"You've come to fight?"

"We come chasing visions, but they have led us here and any enemy of those kidnappers is a friend of ours."

"Kidnappers? You are enemies of the Usurper?"

"The Usurper? Another dark tale come true." The old woman shook her head gravely. "All we know is that we won't put up with another one of our children going missing. They have one of our own. Young Elias is held prisoner. I saw it with my own eyes."

Antimony looked the powerful old woman up and down. He believed her. Fired with emotion, she spoke with a gravitas that made Antimony feel a little like a naughty boy. She had to be genuine.

He nodded to the guards. "Let them in. We must all get inside and lock the gate. I hope Salt and those at the quarry are all right." He turned back to the woman. "Tell me everything you know."

Antimony stood on the roof of the throne room looking out between the tops of the Great Silvers, thankful for the small amount of shelter they offered from the wind, which had been building over the last hour. It blustered past the keep, bringing a cruel chill with it. The mist was thinning as it was stretched and pushed along by the winds, but long streaks of the yellow fog still held their own against the growing gale.

The people in the palace were unnaturally still. Hundreds of motionless figures stood atop the walls or in the compound. Waiting. They had been that way for a couple of hours, but Antimony worried about sending anyone away in case the enemy chose that very moment to attack. So they waited, watching the movements of the enemy under the trees. Occasionally there were gaps in the mist and they caught glimpses of the ranks of enemy soldiers still lining up.

Why weren't they attacking yet?

Three hundred and eighty-two dwarves.

Ninety-six elves.

Two hundred and seventy-three humans.

That's seven hundred and fifty-one...

Fifty-six non-fighters.

That took it down to six hundred and ninety-five defenders. Not everyone was able to fight. Some were too old, others too young, and others were sick or injured. Antimony wished he could stop his brain running through the numbers, but he couldn't when he was nervous. He had never felt this nervous before.

One hundred and sixty-three with real weapons.

Most of the refugee humans didn't have proper weapons. They had grabbed tools or gathered piles of rocks to throw from the walls. Some had slings. Knives had been bound to the ends of sticks to create makeshift spears. It was an admirable, if rather pitiable, effort. But what choice did they have? If the old woman – what was her name again? Hazel Crumpetbottom? – was right, they were severely outnumbered by the Usurper's army.

The first big droplets of rain had begun to fall. Antimony frowned, looking up. The storm that had been brewing had finally decided to break. A flash of lightning illuminated faces full of fear and determination. He wondered how rain might affect the elven bows. Wet strings wouldn't be ideal. But then again, rain would also make climbing the hill to the palace more difficult.

Perhaps the Usurper had thought the same thing. Antimony heard a chilling sound: the distorted blast of a horn that echoed across the Great Forest. For a moment it was drowned out by a rumbling crash of thunder that reverberated through the palace and Antimony's very insides.

The horn came from the south. Antimony hastily crossed to that side, his heart beating fast. Ma was already there. He reached her in time to see ranks of dark-clad soldiers emerging from the forest. Other horns joined with the first. One to the east and then one to the west. They struck a dissonant chord that set Antimony's teeth on edge. More troops marched out of the trees from these directions, surrounding the palace on three sides.

They looked ruthless and confident, in stark contrast to Antimony's group of peasants and craftspeople. They drew up into ranks along the edge of the forest. Antimony couldn't see any of the horses Hazel Crumpetbottom had mentioned. Who knew how many more were hiding in the shelter of the trees? The old woman hadn't been able to count the column in the night-time darkness, but Antimony had quizzed her for details. With what she had said about how long it had taken the column to pass and how fast it was going, Antimony had calculated that they could be facing well over a thousand enemy troops. The Usurper truly had been gathering an army capable of taking over Presadia again. Perhaps the high council had been right, after all, to fear coming here.

Antimony saw Tommarind looking up to him from the southern wall. He was waiting for the command to loose a rain of arrows on the enemy. They were within bowshot, but the elves had a limited supply of arrows.

Ninety-six elves. Approximately fifteen arrows each. That was about one thousand, one hundred and forty arrows.

That wasn't bad. But it would take time to reload and take aim. If the enemy rushed them, each elf might only be able to shoot four or five times before the enemy was at the walls. He didn't want to waste a single arrow until he knew exactly how many enemy soldiers there were.

He delayed giving the signal as long as possible. The Usurper might have done them all kinds of evil, but Antimony didn't want to be the one to start the battle. Perhaps they would be able to talk with the Usurper and prevent it from happening at all.

The horns ceased their long call. The enemy troops beat their weapons and roared, hooted, and howled like animals, a repulsive sound that made Antimony's skin crawl. His hands shook. Oh, how he wished he wasn't in command! Ma was there to help, but the faces around the wall were looking to him. He reached for the pendant of king's glass. He might not feel brave, he might not be a warrior, yet this was what the king had asked him to do, and he would do it.

Gaps appeared in the enemy ranks. Along these corridors, groups carrying wide ladders burst out from the shelter of the trees, racing toward the palace mound at full speed.

There would be no talking, then.

Antimony lifted his hand to give the signal. When he brought it down, ninety-six arrows would rain down upon the enemy.

He stopped himself. The people carrying the ladders were barefoot and poorly clothed. A number were children. As they ran with the ladders toward the palace walls, some of the enemy soldiers shot arrows after them – not to hit them, but to make them run faster.

Antimony hesitated, his arm still raised. If the elves loosed their bows now they would hit the poor people carrying the ladders. These must be the prisoners Hazel Crumpetbottom had told him about. Innocent people and children. One from her own village. What had she called him?

Elias.

He couldn't let the ladders be placed up against the walls, but could he really send down arrows on the heads of these poor prisoners?

27

LADDERS

Hazel Crumpetbottom stood shoulder to shoulder with the ranks of elves, dwarves, and humans, wondering what on earth she had got herself into. Most women of her age would have been relaxing beside a fire, telling stories to their grandchildren. And yet here she was, standing on a wall in the middle of a forest as an evil army descended on her. An army made up of murderous mutants, under the command of an evil elf who had been at the centre of a plot to overthrow the good king, hundreds of years ago.

Well, it was no use grumbling. Here was where she was, so she might as well get on with it.

Even so, Hazel Crumpetbottom had never felt quite so anxious in all her long life. She maintained a confident no-nonsense front in order to calm the fears of the others around her, but her fist was clenched tight around her old staff.

She was proud of her village folk. They had bravely taken their place on the wall. Even though they were farmers, not soldiers, not one had complained about her leading them into this battle. She just prayed to the creator that she hadn't led them all to their deaths.

When the horns sounded, everyone tensed around her.

"Here we go then," she said softly.

People shuffled, trying to peer over the walls. Hazel Crumpetbottom didn't. She was too short to see over the heads of those in front. She would see them soon enough, she was sure. The horns stopped and a guttural war cry erupted from the surrounding forest.

She sniffed. Hmmm. Someone nearby had wet themselves. Well, she couldn't blame them.

Those closest to the edge of the wall, who could see what was happening below, started chattering among themselves, peering down in horror. She wished she could see what all the commotion was about.

A familiar voice cried out in dismay and fear. "Elias! No, Creator, no! Not my boy! Elias!"

It was Gannapple.

"What is it?" she demanded impatiently, using her staff to part the crowd around her so that she could get closer to Gannapple.

"Elias!" Gannapple continued to shout, his voice hoarse, tears gathering in his eyes. Two of the other burly village folk held him back, preventing him from climbing over the edge of the wall.

"It's ladders, Hazel," a Wiggleswandian woman nearer the front told her. Her face was a mask of worry. "They are carried by prisoners. Elias is one of them."

"Creator curse that Usurper!" Hazel Crumpetbottom muttered under her breath.

Tommarind looked to Antimony for the signal. Antimony lifted his arm.

"Draw!" Tommarind bellowed, hearing his command echoed by the captains of the other elves further along the walls. His fifteen archers pulled back their bows and took aim. Tommarind pulled back his own, feeling the strain of the powerful longbow. He didn't aim, but kept his eyes trained on Antimony, waiting for him to drop his hand.

Antimony hesitated.

"Come on, boy," Tommarind muttered, his arms beginning to shake. The elves were experienced archers, and strong, but it was hard work holding a drawn longbow.

"What are you waiting for, Antimony?" he muttered.

Tommarind glanced out over the wall and saw Antimony's dilemma. Instead of enemy soldiers carrying the ladders, there were barefoot humans: men, women, and children. They were unarmed and looked like prisoners, terrified at facing death from both directions. Antimony didn't want to hit them and neither did Tommarind.

"Lower your bows! At ease!" he shouted.

Opal breathed a sigh of relief as the elves lowered their weapons. "Those poor people. Those children," she muttered.

Beside her, Antimony nodded. "He's using them as a human shield. How could he do that?"

"We'll have to try to fend off the ladders from the top."

Her son ran his hands through his dishevelled hair in frustration. She turned to call down through a gap to the group gathered in the large empty room below. One day it would be the throne room, if the palace survived that long. Today it was a command post for Antimony and Opal, and a shelter for those who were unable to fight. It would also be a hospital for anyone who needed it. If the enemy breached the walls it would be a place to fall back to make their final stand. Opal hoped it wouldn't come to that.

Young faces, pale with fear, looked up at her. These were the children she had gathered to act as messengers. They were too young to fight, so Opal had suggested to Antimony that they deliver orders to the defenders on the walls.

"Hello, down there. Do you remember your groups?"

There were nervous nods in response.

"Good, well done. Green group, I need you to run and spread the message. No one is to attack the ladder-carriers. It is vitally important that we push the ladders away, though. Have you got that?"

More nods followed. Opal's heart ached for them. They reminded her of Antimony when he was younger. They should be playing, not taking part in a battle.

"Good. Now hurry along and come back when you're done."

The ladder was getting closer, teetering around like a ship's mast in a storm. Zil didn't actually know what that looked like, but it was how she had imagined it when she'd heard the story about the sailor and the sea monster from the minstrels at the castle. How distant that life now seemed. It had only been a matter of weeks, but it felt like a lifetime.

Not only was her world different, she had changed too. No matter how scared she felt, how out of her depth, she would rather be here on top of this wall than serving wine to a fancy lord, or scrubbing out a disgusting chamber pot.

Further along the wall she heard a man crying out. It was one of the new group who had arrived that morning. He had cracked already. That didn't surprise Zil, but *she* wasn't going to crack. She had been through too much to crack now.

The ladder slammed against the side of the wall with a thud. The ladder-bearers huddled in terror at the base.

"Quick, push it away!" Zil ordered.

She thrust at the ladder with her spear. In reality it was nothing more than a sharpened tent pole, but if one of the enemy came near, she would still poke with it as hard as she could. She could see the soldiers running toward the wall now. Looking to her left and right, Zil saw that more than half the ladders were against the walls. A few had fallen or been knocked away, but metal hooks dropped over the half-finished parapet on impact, making it hard to dislodge them.

"Come on!" she yelled at the man standing next to her, who was staring dumbly at the rushing enemy, frozen in fear. "Help me unhook these. Quickly!"

Antimony stared in horror at the terrible scene before him. All his neat plans, his ideas of how the battle would play out, had been shattered by the ugly reality. Chaos and confusion surrounded him. The elves had shot their volleys of arrows, but only after the ladders had been close enough to the wall that there had been no fear of hitting any of the prisoners.

Now the ladders were hooked over the wall in half a dozen places. A few had already been toppled, but on the western wall the inexperienced refugees defending it had simply fled, leaving a clear space on the wall and an open invitation to the enemy. Fortunately, Tommarind had seen the problem and was making his way along the narrow wall, trying to squeeze past the panicked humans attempting to flee in the other direction.

The enemy troops were climbing the hill as fast as they could, heading straight for the ladders. Some held shields above their heads to protect themselves from the elven arrows and the handful of dwarfish crossbows.

More troops flowed out of the forest – twice as many as Antimony had seen at the beginning; easily the thousand he had predicted, and there was still no sign of the horsemen. What hope did they have in the face of so many?

The first attackers were already close enough to the wall to be hidden from Antimony's view. Another ladder toppled, and Antimony heard the wails of the soldiers who had been in the process of climbing it.

"Antimony!" Ma called from the other side of the keep.

He ran to her.

"Look!" she cried. "Enemy on the eastern wall."

The ladders were wide enough for two soldiers to climb side by side. Two huge brutes wearing animal-skull helmets were just pulling themselves over the top of the wall. They laughed at the valiant but futile attempts of the poorly armed peasants who were attempting to beat them away with sticks and rocks. Then an old woman – Antimony was sure it was Hazel Crumpetbottom – ran at them, swinging her stick like a quarterstaff. It connected with one of the enemy soldier's heads. He snarled with anger.

"Are the reserves still below, Ma?"

Antimony had decided to keep back a small group of dwarves with fighting experience, under the command of Granite Greybeard, the formidable high council member. With such inexperienced and poorly armed defenders on the wall, he had wanted ready reinforcements on standby.

"Yes, they're awaiting orders."

"Good. Tell Granite to go to the eastern wall. Tommarind will deal with the western wall."

"I'll pass on the word," said Opal. She was cool and calm, her experience as a soldier evident. Antimony, meanwhile, was a nervous wreck as he watched his friends risk their lives. Ma had insisted he would be more help up here, where they could survey the whole battle, but he couldn't help feeling like a coward, leaving his friends and the poorly armed villagers to fight off the Usurper's army.

Hazel Crumpetbottom swung her staff again, spinning it with such speed and force that when it connected with the ugly scoundrel's head, he stumbled backwards in shock. Beside her, the distraught Gannapple roared. He was a large, strong man, and he was running full speed toward the ladder, an unstoppable force. The man Hazel Crumpetbottom had hit with her staff looked up in surprise as the fearless father crashed into him like a landslide.

Gannapple's weight pushed the man backwards and he crashed over the parapet and onto his comrades who were still climbing the ladder. Unfortunately, the force of his attack carried Gannapple over with him. Perhaps it was what he had intended all along in his desperation to reach Elias. His momentum caused the ladder to topple away from the wall.

Hazel Crumpetbottom launched herself forward to grab Gannapple and prevent him from being carried completely over the edge. The ladder teetered upright for a moment before falling back into the mass of the enemy army below.

This would have been all very well and good, thought Hazel Crumpetbottom, if Gannapple had not still been clinging to the ladder and she to him. She found herself stretched out over nothing, her tiptoes on the top of the wall and her hands hanging on to Gannapple, who in turn clung to the back of the ladder.

Oh dear, she thought, as her toes slid away from the wall.

28

MUD AND WATER

Hazel Crumpetbottom was too old for this. No respectable woman of her age should be flying through the air above an army of brigands, or falling into an undignified tangle of stinking soldiers in the mud and rain.

And that had only been the start! Thankfully, their fall had been cushioned by the soldiers below. They had tumbled off the ladder and slid down the hill along with the confused enemy soldiers. Covered from head to foot in squelching mud, they had barely escaped being trampled to death.

The mud, it turned out, had been their friend. Once Hazel Crumpetbottom had untangled herself from the pile of people at the bottom of the hill, she looked around for the dazed Gannapple, who was barely distinguishable from the others around him, thanks to the mud. Grabbing his arm, she'd yanked him into the shelter of the trees. The enemy's attention was on the ladders and the defenders. No one glanced twice at the two additional muddy figures. What would any of the defenders be doing outside the walls, after all?

There was no way for them to get back inside the walls, and staying out in the open only increased the chances of someone noticing that they were not part of the army.

Hazel Crumpetbottom looked around, wondering what to do next. The enemy looked far less scary from down here. Up on the wall they had looked as if they knew what they were doing. Down here they seemed almost as disorganized and unprepared as the defenders.

There were a lot more of them, though. The soldiers were an unlikely mix of all kinds of people and races, and most were rough: the sort of no good'uns who only looked out for themselves and didn't mind who they hurt along the way.

Their weapons and equipment were in a bad way, rusty and worn. This wasn't a disciplined and well-organized army, but a group of violent ruffians who had been pointed at the palace and let loose.

"Come on, Gannapple. Let's get deeper into the wood. I can't believe the mess you've got us into. If we ever get back to Wiggleswand, I swear I'll be giving you chores for a year."

"Elias..." the poor man said, looking at her with sad longing in his eyes. "I must find Elias."

She fixed the desperate father with one of her best stares. It didn't work; his pain and pleading remained. She cursed herself for a fool.

"Oh, very well. In for an apple, in for an orchard. But I'm making it two years of chores!"

Tommarind pulled the last arrow from his quiver. He had used them sparingly. The battle had been raging for well over an hour now. It was hard to tell exactly how long, particularly in the dim, unnatural twilight beneath the storm clouds.

The rain was hammering down. It wasn't refreshing rain, but a heavy downpour that drenched defenders and attackers alike. The smooth new stone was slippery underfoot, and Tommarind's bowstring was wet through. He was just grateful he didn't have hair. The humans and dwarves had to keep pulling it away from their eyes, only to have the rain plaster it flat again moments later.

After the initial rush it had been an endless task of racing back and forth along the wall, fending off renewed attempts from the enemy to hook their ladders over the wall. In the rare moments when there was not a ladder within easy reach, Tommarind had taken the chance to send his arrows down on the enemy below. But it was like spitting into an ocean. There were so many more of them; they were like a swarm of angry ants.

Each time a ladder hooked into place, the enemy would rush up, bringing the fight onto the walls. Here the defenders lost all their advantage. While the enemy troops were below, even an untrained peasant could throw rocks at them, although they had now run out of those. On the wall, the rebels' better weapons and greater experience turned that advantage on its head. Tommarind had saved more than one doomed human and dwarfish stonecutter, but the elves couldn't be everywhere at once.

He heard the clang of another ladder to his left. Then almost immediately he heard two more to his right. He turned to look. Three ladders at once.

"Ladders! Stop the ladders!" he called, his voice hoarse from shouting. He raced toward the nearest one, but the enemy troops had already swarmed up and were nearing the top.

Tommarind drew his large knife.

Zil poked and prodded, smacked and swung with her sharpened stick. It wouldn't be that deadly in a proper fight, but it was effective at making life more difficult for a heavily laden enemy soldier trying to climb a rickety ladder.

She had managed to organize the fearful workers around her into teams. They were working together to push the ladders away, and were successfully keeping their little section clear. Antimony had told Zil to keep an eye on the wooden gate below to her left. Some of the soldiers had been hacking away at it with axes, but Zil's team had discouraged them with rocks and arrows. Besides, Antimony had known the gate would be the weakest point and had had it made of thick, hard wood, with lots of bolts and braces. It would take them a while yet to break through. Perhaps the Usurper thought the ladders would be quicker.

Unfortunately, there was little they could do to defend the gate now. They had run out of rocks to rain down on the attackers. The elves who had been closest had moved further down the wall to help in the fight there.

Zil looked out during a momentary lull, when no new ladders were threatening their section. There was a disturbance in the enemy ranks that made her groan. This wasn't good.

A group were running toward the wooden gate carrying the trunk of a tree between them, a dozen huge men on either side. A spiked steel helmet had been hammered into the leading end. That would make short work of the gate, particularly since it had already been weakened by the axes.

She glanced up to the keep to see if Antimony had spotted the new threat. She couldn't see him or Opal. She would have to take matters into her own hands.

"They're attacking the gate. We can't let them get in. Can you hold the wall?" she called to two of her small groups.

They answered with frightened but determined nods.

"Good. You there, run to the keep and tell Antimony or Opal that they have a battering ram. Everyone else come with me."

She skidded along the slippery wall, pushing her wet hair away from her eyes. A mean-looking rusty blade lay where it had been dropped as a ladder had been pushed back. Zil grabbed it. It was heavier than she had expected.

She wished the stupid rain would stop so she could see more clearly. The wind had been growing ever stronger. It whipped the raindrops up and slammed them into her numb face. Reaching the inner ladder, she clambered down into the workers' camp. Her little crew followed. None of them were soldiers. She knew some of them from the castle, where they had been servants together – a baker, another maid, and two stable boys – and the others were village folk or farmers. She had no idea what they could do to defend the door, but someone had to do something.

She reached the bottom, slipping in the mud. "Come on, we need to reinforce the gate. Get anything you can find; the bigger the better."

The furniture and other odd scraps they began stacking against the gate wouldn't hold for long, she knew, but it might slow the rebels down once they got through. They raced back and forth, piling whatever they could find against the door: benches, tent poles, blocks of stone, and timber beams.

Boom.

Zil heard the first crash of the battering ram against their door, followed by an ominous cracking sound.

Antimony ran his hands through his hair. His lips moved with constant calculations, but they helped to calm him.

The situation was desperate. The walls had been breached in six different places now, and the defenders were fighting back with mixed success. Antimony had heard the battering ram before he had seen it, and before Zil's messenger arrived. Rushing across, he had been just in time to see the door begin to splinter under the second ram. Quick-witted Zil had managed to gather a group who were throwing anything they could find in front of the door. Perhaps it would give them a minute or two longer before the door gave way, but not much more.

"Antimony," Ma said at his shoulder, her voice grave. "We are overwhelmed. There are simply too many of them. I think we need to pull everyone back to the keep."

Numbers and probabilities were racing through Antimony's head, all of which told him she was right. They had lost the wall, their best line of defence. All they could do was pull back to the keep to make a final stand.

He nodded, sick to his stomach. "OK. Give the signal."

Ma gave him a tight-lipped grimace. "There's nothing more you could have done, Antimony. There are simply too many of them, and our people are farmers and craftspeople, not soldiers."

Antimony watched as Ma turned and made her way toward the beacon at the centre of the keep. She drew back the canvas covering, revealing a pile of oil-soaked wood, before lighting the signal with her lantern. For a moment the flames looked weak, and Antimony thought they wouldn't take, but then the oil caught and the fire burst upwards in spite of the rain.

It flared, bright and bold in the grey storm. The red flames licked at the raindrops and made them hiss. They wouldn't last long. When the oil was spent, the pounding rain would quickly extinguish them, but it would be enough to tell the defenders to pull back.

Antimony wasn't sure what good it would do, but the king had charged him to protect his palace and his people, and that's what he would do. To the very end.

29

KNIGHT OF PRESADIA

"Come in, quickly! You're the last," said Antimony, ushering the final few fleeing defenders into the large throne room. He looked at the terrified people, packed shoulder to shoulder. The teardrop-shaped windows gave a dim grey illumination to the frightened and demoralized crowd within. Each time the lightning flashed, he could see the exhausted faces of the wretched people who had been entrusted to him by the king. A poor job he had done of protecting them.

Antimony could hear crying and worried murmurs, whispered words and the groans of those who had been hurt in the fight. The Usurper's army flooded into the palace through the breached gate and up the ladders.

Someone had given Antimony a sword – an ugly rusted blade that had belonged to one of the enemy. It felt large and unnatural in his right hand.

"Granite, Ma, Tommarind, everyone is inside. Pull back!"

The fearsome trio – three unlikely yet formidable warriors – had protected the way into the keep for the retreating workers. The other elves were on the roof, using the last few arrows to keep the attackers back from the door. Antimony spared a fleeting thought for Sparks, wondering where she had gone. Perhaps she would return from her hunting to find nothing but ruins and dead bodies. It was sad to think he might never see her again.

A group led by Zil dragged a barricade across the arched doorway, sealing in the defenders as best they could. Antimony had kept the most experienced soldiers near the door to repel any further attack for as long as possible.

In silence, they watched through the frame of the large doorway as the enemy troops poured through the broken gate and along the tops of the walls. They had ropes and nets, and he wondered what they were planning to do. Like a black wave, they broke over the camp, smashing and looting. The defenders, huddling between the Great Silvers, listened to the destruction with horror. Everyone knew that when the enemy soldiers' greed was satisfied and their fun was over, they would turn their attention to the keep.

There was a thunder of hooves as a party of mounted soldiers rode through the smashed gate. Antimony saw Wolf-ear and his unsavoury companions among them, but his attention was drawn to one he hadn't seen before but whose identity was unmistakable: a blood-red elf. He wore a crown fashioned from a jawbone with vicious teeth that jutted up like cruel spikes. Where the traditional elven tattoos would once have been, there was scarred skin. He wore a suit of black armour and rode the largest horse Antimony had ever seen.

One of the mounted party blew a horn and the pillaging soldiers turned reluctantly from what they were doing to look at their king. A strange hush fell over the palace compound. Only the hammering rain and claps of thunder dared to compete with the thud of the Usurper's horse's hooves, though even these seemed to dull in response to his arrival.

They neared the entrance to the keep, and the scarlet elf reined in his horse. The group looked around. The Usurper's troops watched him with part reverence and part wariness.

He surveyed the scene with apparent pleasure before raising his voice. It was calm, beguiling even, at odds with his appearance and the fear in his followers' faces. Despite the softness of his tone and the hammering of the rain, it carried through the stormy palace compound clear and strong.

"Well done, my little beasts," he congratulated his soldiers.

They stood taller at their lord's pleasure, lapping up his praise like loyal dogs. The Rebel Elf turned to examine the part-grown keep.

"I thought I had killed these filthy trees centuries ago. They always remind me of the Silverwood." He saw Antimony and his friends watching from the doorway. "Ah. Howell, where are you?"

Wolf-ear jerked in his saddle before moving to his king's side. Antimony noticed that the man's other ear, the one his axe had nicked during their last encounter, had also been replaced with the hairy, pointed ear of a wolf. Blood and pus oozed from the clumsy stitches.

"This must be the boy leader and his merry band that you told me about. Really! I don't know why you've been making such a fuss about them. You saw their laughable attempt to defend themselves. They're peasants and pushovers, nothing more."

"Yes, King Kalithor. But you can see how much they have rebuilt and how many there were. If you hadn't dealt with them, who knows—"

"Don't dare to lecture me, dog."

Wolf-ear lowered his head. "Sorry, my lord."

"As it happens, though, you are right. This... *palace*," he spat the word, "may not look like much, but it stands for that useless excuse for a king. I cannot let Presadia unite under that banner again and repeat the mistakes of the past."

He turned from Wolf-ear to look out over his army, lifting his voice.

"Presadia lies in squalor. Its people are pathetic and weak. The old king encouraged humility and love," his tone was mocking, "but these traits do not build a strong kingdom. The humble are trampled upon. Love does not get what it wants. A strong nation is made up of strong people; people who are not afraid to take what they desire; people who refuse to be trampled on. The strongest will rise to the top. Those who desire it can have unlimited pleasure. You can live like kings yourselves.

"But for this to happen, Presadia needs a strong ruler. A firm ruler. One who will bring progress and let industry flourish. One who will not demand love, only obedience. That one is me. I, King Kalithor, will unite Presadia! I, King Kalithor, will free Presadia! I, King Kalithor, will rule Presadia!"

His followers whooped, howled, and barked, some even dropping onto all fours like the beasts they modelled themselves after. The Usurper let the depraved racket continue for a few moments before lifting his hand for silence.

He turned to look through the entrance to the throne room, at Antimony and his friends. "So, this is him? The boy who leads this rabble?"

Antimony's arms tingled. Blood pounded in his ears. He drew a deep breath and reached up to touch the pendant the king had given him, hoping it would bring him the courage and boldness he didn't feel.

"I am Antimony, a knight of the true king of Presadia."

The words felt silly as they slipped off his tongue. The Usurper must have thought so too, as he laughed spitefully.

"Ha! I can almost believe it. He always did like to choose the feeble. But the king is gone, boy. He ran away years ago. He's either dead, or afraid of ever returning to Presadia. If he did, I would finish what I started. This forest is mine. No child playing knights and heroes can change that. I destroyed this palace once, and I will take great pleasure in doing it again."

"This is the king's palace. You are not welcome here."

"*I* am the only king now. You have spirit, I'll give you that. But you must see how hopeless your position is. I will tear this place down again, and we will kill you all. Unless…" The Usurper paused, as if considering the options. "I'll give you one chance to save everyone; all of your people. No one else needs to die."

Antimony was taken aback. The weight of responsibility for the workers rested heavily on his shoulders. If he could save them all…

"Pledge yourselves to me, each and every one of you. I have been preparing for a long time to conquer Presadia. The time has now come, and she is ripe for the taking. Serve me and you will live. Serve me well and I will give you riches and rewards beyond your wildest imagination. You will be lords and ladies in my new realm. All I require is total loyalty and commitment. Anyone who defies me, I will kill. What's more, I will kill everyone they care for too. Mercy was the old king's weakness. Trusting people to obey out of love is why he was overthrown. I do not have these weaknesses. You have one chance, and one chance only."

Pledge himself to the Usurper? Antimony recoiled. The very one who had led the rebellion to overthrow the king? A few simple words would save them, but at what cost?

"Give me your answer."

The mathematical equation was simple. A few words in exchange for his life and the lives of all his people. And yet… He had pledged himself to the king.

Serving me won't be easy… It may demand even your life. The words echoed in his head, as real as if the king were speaking them beside him.

215

Antimony breathed deeply and recalled the words of his pledge. "I am a knight of the true king; a representative of his rule and reign. I stand for him alone. I am charged to defend the defenceless, lift up the downtrodden and speak up for those who have no voice. I have pledged to free the oppressed and welcome in the lonely. I have chosen him, the real king of Presadia, above all other lords and kings. I cannot – I will not – pledge myself to any other."

"You are a fool, boy! You choose to die rather than serve me? Fine. I will kill you and everyone with you."

He turned to his troops.

"Wait!" Antimony shouted.

His mind skimmed back through a book he had read long ago: a book of legends and stories from the time after the king's exile; a dark time when battles and armies had been commonplace, as greedy people fought to fill the void.

"What about battle by champion?"

"Battle by champion? What do you take me for, boy? What would I stand to gain? I can kill you all here and now. You are no threat to me. Your offer is more foolish than your pathetic loyalty to a worthless king."

"Will you accept? One champion from each side. If we win, you let us go free without our allegiance."

"Of course I don't agree," the Usurper spat.

"King Kalithor?" Wolf-ear interjected.

"What is it, Howell?"

"Are you not in the mood for some light entertainment, my lord? I would willingly act as your champion, if you will let me fight that little boy. I want to repay him for what he did to my ear. It would be fun. He is no threat to me."

The Usurper considered Wolf-ear's words, looking Antimony up and down with an amused grin.

"Very well, Howell. You are right. It would be fun to watch the little knight die."

"So you accept?" Antimony asked, wondering what he was doing. He didn't stand a chance against Wolf-ear. The man was huge and burly, not to mention an experienced fighter. He wore thick armour, and his sword looked comfortable and deadly in his grip. Antimony was gangly and thin. He had no muscles to speak of and he had no idea how to wield the rusty sword he had just been given. But it was all he could do. He couldn't pledge himself to Kalithor; he already belonged to the true king.

Antimony's brain calculated the probabilities. It took no mathematical ability to work out that he would lose. It wasn't even likely that the Usurper would keep his word if he won. But no matter how low the probability, when all other options were exhausted, even the slightest of chances was mathematically better than rolling over and letting everyone be slaughtered.

He stepped forward and readied himself to climb over the barricade.

"Ha! As I said, you have spirit. You would have done well with me. I accept, on the condition that no one here helps you. If I see a single dwarf, human or elf move as much as a finger you will all die immediately."

"Agreed."

"Antimony." Ma grabbed his shoulder, desperation on her face. "What are you doing?"

"Ma, I have to. We have no other options."

"But he'll kill you."

"They'll kill us all anyway. I know I don't stand a chance, but what else can I do?" Her eyes were brimming with tears. He didn't often look people directly in the eye. It made him uncomfortable. But now, he looked deep into the eyes of the one who loved him more than anyone else.

"You truly are my mother. I wish I'd known about everything, but… I love you very much and I'm sorry I ran off. I–"

"I love you, Antimony," she interrupted, drawing him into a hug that squeezed the breath from him. "That's all that matters right now. I love you. You are my son. And I am so very proud of you."

"The king would be proud of you too, Antimony," Tommarind told him. "You have reminded us again of what it means to follow him." The elf placed his hand on the ground, squelching it deep into the mud. "May mother earth uphold you and give you strength."

"Thank you, Tommarind. I think I'm going to need it!"

"You can do it, Antimony," Zil said with a confidence that almost persuaded Antimony she believed it. "You show him! Thank you for… for all of this. Even now I wouldn't change any of it for the world."

Antimony didn't reply. Even if he'd wanted to, the words were stuck in his throat. Trying to force them out would release the pent-up fear and emotion that had filled him to bursting. All he could do was nod, before climbing over the barricade.

30

FIRE AND HONOUR

Sparks soared above the world, enjoying the sensation of flight. This was what she had been made for. All those eons of being trapped in the body of a worm with a dull mind. This was freedom; this was life.

She swerved to avoid a large patch of thick yellow cloud. She had quickly learned that these were bad, making her lungs hurt and her still-soft scales itch. The rain also stung a little. Something inside her knew that it was not pure and clean, as it should be.

But her inner fire burned bright. It kept her warm in the stormy conditions and its energy made her feel stronger with each passing wingbeat.

She felt a tug of something. It wasn't a sensation like the other sensations. It wasn't touch or sight or smell, but something deeper; something more inexplicable in her developing mind.

"Hmmmm," she growled, trying to interpret the feeling. "An-tim-ony."

The kind one.

He was in trouble.

Wolf-ear's first downward stroke hit Antimony's upheld sword like a blacksmith's hammer. Antimony stumbled back under the force of the blow, his arm numbed. It was all he could do to stop his own sword rebounding into his face.

Wolf-ear laughed. Swinging his blade casually, he sauntered toward Antimony once again. The Usurper and his troops jeered at Antimony's pathetic attempts to fight off Wolf-ear's blows. It was one big game to them. They knew he was no threat to their champion.

Wolf-ear was toying with him, clearly enjoying humiliating him. Well, humiliation didn't matter to Antimony if it prevented harm coming to the workers, even if only for a few minutes.

He could already feel himself tiring and he hadn't managed a single attack against his opponent. He was too busy defending himself from the continuous blows raining down. How did the man swing the heavy blade with such ease and strength?

The rain wasn't helping. Antimony blinked water from his eyes. Every strike caused him to stumble and slide in the thick mud and puddles.

Wolf-ear struck him again, harder this time, and Antimony barely managed to raise his sword to defend himself. Wolf-ear's sword slid down Antimony's, slamming into the guard with such force that Antimony let go. The sword splashed into a puddle and Antimony's feet slipped out from under him. He fell hard on his back in a muddy puddle.

Wolf-ear laughed again, kicking out at Antimony's flailing legs.

"Finish him, my little wolf," the Usurper shouted over the din of jeering and the buffeting rain. "I tire of the tiny knight."

"With pleasure," Wolf-ear growled. He raised his head to howl an imitation of his favoured totem.

His howl was answered by a screeching roar. A blur of scarlet swept out of nowhere. Wolf-ear was knocked clean off his feet, falling back into the group of horsemen.

The horses reared and bucked in terror at Sparks' dramatic appearance. The nearby enemy soldiers scurried back to avoid the screaming dragon. She stood between Antimony and the army, her glittering scales bright and vivid against the mud-covered surroundings. She drew in a deep breath before releasing one of her small globules of flame. It exploded on some of the nearby soldiers, who climbed over each other to get out of the way, throwing themselves down to roll on the wet ground in a bid to extinguish the flames.

"Idiots!" the Usurper cried, reining in his own terrified horse. "You know what to do. The nets! The nets!"

Antimony scrambled to his feet, backing up to stand near the door to the keep, away from Sparks' swishing, spiky tail.

The angry dragon might have been small, but she was brave, spitting out fire and roaring her challenge. For a minute or two it worked; there was total confusion. Then the Usurper's army regained their wits. Their scouts had prepared them for the presence of the baby dragon, and the nets they had brought with them were thrown. They were weighted at the edges and tangled around the dragon's small spikes, her thrashing head, and fragile wings. Sparks tore at them angrily with her small teeth, twisting in frustration at the cords as they entangled her.

More nets were thrown, binding her tighter. Antimony rushed out to try to help her, but the frantic dragon was twisting and writhing too much for him to get close. She tried to open her wings and take flight, but this only tangled her further, and all she managed was a lurching half-jump before sprawling to the floor.

She thrashed about and breathed more fire. This freed her head, but nothing else. She snapped and roared in frustration at the enemy soldiers who were rushing in to tie her down with ropes secured to the ground with wooden pegs pushed into the soft mud.

"Ah! The dragon my scouts told me so much about. I wondered

when it would come. I thought they had been lying." He examined the small dragon. "What a feisty little creature it is. I haven't seen a dragon for a very long time. It's not very big, is it? I'm sure I can find a way to put this beast to work, though. A dragon might be useful to me."

The Usurper had to shout to make himself heard over the dragon's roars and a rising wind that was now whipping the rain painfully into Antimony's face.

"An-tim-ony," Sparks whimpered.

"Sparks!" Antimony looked helplessly at the trapped creature, his voice torn away by the wind.

"Now, I know I didn't mention dragons specifically," said Kalithor, "but I think this still counts as cheating. You were to fight alone. You have lost. And now you will die."

The Usurper drew his own sword. He kicked his jittery horse forward. Antimony looked up as his end approached.

The pendant grew hot beneath his clothes. The ground began to vibrate, and the sky to the north lit up with a flash, like brilliant lightning. Unlike lightning, however, it didn't fade. It lit the storm clouds from within, making them glow brightly enough to cast shadows in the palace many miles away. It reflected off the armour and swords of the gathered host. The reflections grew in intensity, flickering with half-seen pictures and places, visions and faces, myriads of images showing the deep wounds of Presadia. The reflections bloomed with vividness.

Was this what people meant, thought Antimony, *when they talked about your life flashing before your eyes?* Then he saw that everyone had stopped to stare in bewilderment at the reflections.

The king's pendant burned against Antimony's chest. He tugged it out and stared into its glowing depths. He saw a mountaintop crowned with huge crystals that shone brighter than the sun. A tornado of blackness swirled over the mountain. Antimony sensed rather than saw a figure at the centre of the cyclone before the visions became too bright to look at.

The king.

The sky to the north grew brighter. Everyone turned to watch, lifting their arms to shade their eyes, squinting against the awesome light and the spinning reflections that flickered across every raindrop, puddle, and piece of metal.

A vast shape obscured the sky, silhouetted against the dazzling white clouds. It stretched as wide as the palace itself and crashed toward them with terrible finality. Presadia was being torn apart. The very sky was falling, shattering into dazzling greens and yellows. A wall of ruby flame descended, as hot as a furnace. Antimony stumbled back into the shelter of the keep.

He closed his eyes and waited for the end of the world to happen.

31

For the King

"Karagnoord greets you, little one," the dragon roared at Sparks as he landed.

The heavens had exploded with light only moments before. Karagnoord had not needed to look north to know the significance of the moment. Dragons felt these things in a way other species never could.

The newly pupated dragon, a little red thing with the scent of magma, was tangled in spindly, mortal-made ropes. It shamed Karagnoord to see one of his sisters humiliated in such a fashion. The shame fed his anger, stoking the fire in his belly and heating his tongue until it burned painfully in his mouth. He roared with fury, releasing another deadly cloud of flame on the evil-smelling horde who had dared to desecrate this sacred place. Swinging his head around, he bathed the young dragon with the last vestiges of his fire. It was not hot enough to hurt her; in fact, being of the magma variety she would most likely enjoy it. Still, it was hot enough to incinerate the ropes and nets that trapped her.

"There you are, my little friend. That is no place for a dragon."

"Mmmmm," the young dragon replied thankfully. Her speech had clearly not fully developed yet.

"Do you have a name, sister?"

"Hmmmm. S-par-ks," she croaked.

An unusual name for a dragon. A mortal-sounding name. But if she had chosen it, he would not question it.

"Well then, Sparks, learn from me how a dragon fights."

When the world didn't end, Antimony opened his eyes.

The sky had dimmed, the reflections had faded, and his pendant was cool again. Despite that, the scene before him was unrecognizable from only moments earlier. Those belonging to the Usurper's army were fighting among themselves in their desperate attempts to flee. Filling a large part of the palace compound was the biggest creature Antimony had ever seen. It was an enormous dragon, resplendent in green and yellow scales. It must have been almost twice the size of Khoree.

He was decimating the enemy ranks. Beside one of his gargantuan claws the tiny Sparks mimicked the great dragon's attacks, thrashing her neck back and forth to snap at the Usurper's troops, swiping her viciously spiked tail in a deadly arc and occasionally burping fire.

The Usurper's foot soldiers were in a frenzy, many fleeing toward the entrance. The Usurper and his company of horsemen were fully preoccupied with trying to stay on their petrified horses.

None of Antimony's calculations had accounted for this turn of events. With the vivid image of the shining mountaintop and the king of Presadia clear in his mind, Antimony turned to face the doorway of the keep and the dumbstruck faces within.

He thrust his sword in the air. "For the king!"

Then he turned and ran toward the Usurper and his men. Before he had taken more than a couple of steps, he heard the shouts of his friends repeating the battle cry. Soon Antimony was propelled by the tumultuous cheer of the entire keep.

The dragons were herding the enemy army into a group on one side of the palace compound. The group of horsemen around the Usurper had managed to control their mounts enough to try to make a break for the entrance. Antimony wasn't going to let them escape. He ran as fast as he could, trying to block their way and turn the anxious horses aside. They quickly outpaced him. Just as Antimony thought they would escape, they reared up short. Through the shattered gates, a figure on a long-haired pony galloped into view.

"Salt!" he exclaimed, relieved to see his friend safe and well.

Behind Salt were more dwarves, all mounted, impressive in their gleaming suits of armour. They passed through the gate as more dwarves flooded through on foot. Reinforcements had arrived from Val-Chasar.

Along with the dwarves was a curious group of barefooted humans armed with salvaged weapons and led by an old woman. Hazel Crumpetbottom! Antimony had no idea how or why she had come to be outside the palace gates, but there she was, leading the former ladder-carrying prisoners, who were no longer helpless and enslaved. Everything had changed so quickly that Antimony's mind couldn't keep up.

The Usurper's horsemen wheeled around, trapped between Antimony and his friends, the two deadly dragons, and the new army that had closed off their only means of escape.

Rage and hatred turned the Usurper's face an even darker shade of red. His eyes burned with fury and frustration.

"Surrender!" Antimony shouted, pulling up to stand just a stone's throw from him. "Surrender, and remain here as my prisoner to face the king's judgment."

"Never!" The Usurper turned his horse to gallop directly at Antimony, sword raised ready to strike him down.

Time slowed as Antimony's brain calculated his chances. The speed of acceleration, the distance between them, the arc of the blade...

Suddenly, the Rebel Elf was gone. Faster than Antimony could have imagined possible for a creature of his size, the huge green-yellow dragon had slammed a claw against the galloping rider. Horse and elf were knocked aside as easily as Antimony might bat away an annoying mine-moth. The dragon pinned the renegade elf beneath his claw. He lowered his muzzle to sniff the struggling elf before snorting with disgust.

"I know you," the dragon said. "Kalithor. You served the king right here in the palace. I heard about what you did. You are a traitor. You turned against your king and against Presadia. You have caused misery and untold damage. You shame the noble elven race, and you disgust me. I would eat you right here, only I couldn't stomach the foul taste."

Antimony blinked. Brushes with death were becoming almost second nature to him now.

"Thank you, er, Dragon. I'm Antimony. I'm... well, I've been in charge of rebuilding the palace. Thank you f-for your help."

"My name is Karagnoord. My sister here holds you in high regard. I can sense her affection for you. As for thanks, it is not needed. This elf deserves everything he gets. I agree with your judgment. He must face the king's justice. All of these vermin must. I will watch this one personally." He turned back to snarl at the struggling Usurper.

"Antimony!" Zil threw herself at him. "We did it! *You* did it!"

He turned in time to be caught in a hug of joy that surprised him. Awkward and unsure of how to respond, he found himself enjoying it at the same time. He liked Zil. A lot. Thankfully, he didn't have to think of the correct response, as he was snatched from Zil by Ma, who buried him in a more maternal embrace.

"A knight of Presadia you might be, but today I saw my son all grown up. I'm so proud of you, Antimony, my love."

"Ma…"

He didn't need to say anything else. There were still more questions than answers. The knowledge that he was adopted still left a gap he felt he needed to fill, but that gap was not a lack of love or belonging. He couldn't have found more love anywhere than in this small, formidable, devoted dwarf. The gap in his history was not a gap in himself. He was as whole and complete as he needed to be.

The gap was like the cracks in the mirror portal, or the unfinished work on the palace. In a perfect world, it wouldn't have been there. But in the imperfect world they lived in, it provided a chance for the love and care that filled those cracks to shine out strongly. Perhaps cracks that had been repaired were no less beautiful than the unblemished original.

Antimony held Ma. His ma. He didn't feel like a man, or a leader, or a hero from the legends. In that moment, all he felt like was a son; loved and valued. That was worth more to him than anything else.

32

THE THRONE ROOM

The rain had stopped. The storm had subsided as abruptly as the battle. The ground was still muddy, but the weather was almost the exact opposite of the day before. Bright sunlight shone down on the palace, bathing the workers in its warm rays. It was perhaps the clearest, most pleasant day Antimony had ever known. The sky was blue, and the sounds of the forest had returned. The weather was warm with a light breeze, but the air tasted crystal clear. There was no sign of the yellow fog. It felt as if the world was new.

Antimony looked at the palace, squinting in the bright sunshine. For a moment it almost seemed to glow white, and he thought he could see the turrets with their bejewelled spires, and the great keep made from the silver trees, rising to staggering heights. The flight of fancy passed, and Antimony found himself looking at the real thing again.

It wasn't quite finished yet. There were no bejewelled turrets and the keep still had a considerable amount of growing to do. The gate was an empty gap, now cleared of the splintered wood, and the walls were undressed – not the gleaming whitewashed circle they would one day be. It wasn't the perfect result Antimony so longed to see, but it still pointed to what it would one day be, while its scars told something of where it had come from, and how it had stood firm and proud against all odds.

It was evening time when Khoree the dragon was spotted on the horizon. As she landed in the palace compound, Antimony saw she had passengers wedged between the spikes that ran down her spine. Antimony couldn't see Summer and Jonah, but High Lord Tin was there, along with a beautiful female elf and the king himself. Remarkably, Tin's immensely long and impressive beard was no longer silver but a luxurious gold.

Murmurs of excitement rippled through the crowd with the arrival of the king. He still had on the shabby rags Antimony recognized, but he now also wore a crown of breath-taking beauty; a masterpiece of craftsmanship, made of four strands: silver, iron, gemstones, and the white wood of the Great Silvers. It reminded Antimony of the palace, with a different section for each of the four races, all woven together in unity to create something wonderful.

The people gathered to watch the king dismount. He looked around at the palace, a wide smile on his face. Antimony, surrounded by Ma, Zil, Tommarind, Salt and, for some reason, Hazel Crumpetbottom, walked over to welcome him.

Khoree stretched before stamping her way over to meet Sparks and greet Karagnoord. Behind the king, Tin and the elf also dismounted and followed at a respectful distance. Tin winked at Antimony, the small action helping to calm the butterflies in his stomach.

"Antimony!" said the king. "My faithful knight. It is very good to see you again. It looks as if you have been busy since we last met."

"Your majesty." Antimony bowed awkwardly. That was what you were supposed to do in front of royalty, after all. "Welcome to… your palace."

The king laughed at Antimony's nerves, but not in a way that made him self-conscious. Quite the opposite, in fact. It made Antimony relax and laugh too.

"It has been a long time since I last stood inside these walls. You have done an excellent job. It is beautiful."

"I'm sorry it's not finished. It's not like it's meant to be. We–"

"Antimony, calm yourself. There is no need to apologize. I love a work in progress – I've told you that before. What all of you have done is remarkable. And besides, I have been in exile for a long time. I have much to attend to before I can enjoy the luxury of sitting around in my palace. You still have time to finish it for me."

"You want us to keep going?"

"Of course. Why not? You and anyone who wants to help. And when you are done, you are all welcome to live here if you wish, or you may go back to your homes. Now I have returned, I will bring peace and prosperity back to every corner of Presadia."

He looked around at the crowds gathered nearby.

"My lord, before that…"

"Yes, Antimony?"

"The Usurper and what's left of his army are over there with the dragons. What do you want us to do with them?"

"They tried to drive me from my own kingdom, but now they will be exiled from Presadia. It will be a true exile – so far away that their wickedness will affect no one but themselves. They have chosen to set themselves against me and my kingdom, so I will give them what they desire: a place without me, or the beauty and goodness of Presadia. You have a portal in the quarry, I believe?"

"Yes. It goes to Val-Chasar."

"For now it does. Later I will use it to send them far away from Presadia, where they will cause no more trouble for anyone. But before that I would like to see the work you have done here."

"Of course. There's not really much to see at the moment."

"And yet I would see it," said the king, giving Antimony another warm smile.

"Before you do, your highness," High Lord Tin interjected, "may I say hello to my cousin's husband's sister's son?"

The dwarf gave Antimony a mighty bear hug.

"Well, my boy! It looks like you have been very busy in my absence. I thought I had stories to tell you, but it looks as if I'm not the only one who's had an adventure."

"It didn't really feel like an adventure most of the time. It's all just happened, really." Antimony peered around him. "Where are Summer and Jonah? Where did you go and what under earth has happened to your beard?"

Tin chuckled. "Slow down, Antimony, lad. There's plenty of time to tell you the whole story – just as I hope you'll tell me yours. In a bat-nutshell, we found the king, as you can see. He helped the children return to their world. I already miss them. I don't mind telling you it was quite the journey. This new beard will never let me forget. I never thought I would make it back. But we did, and with the king, no less!"

"What?"

"Hush now, Antimony. There will be plenty of time for catching up. I can introduce you to Ellenair, too." Salt indicated the beautiful elf who had accompanied them. "Now we have a wedding to plan as well. But you don't want to keep our king waiting. I promise I'll tell you everything over dinner."

Antimony nodded, reluctantly letting his hundred and one questions remain unasked.

Instead, he invited the king on a tour of the palace, leading him around the camp to see the construction in progress. The king looked with interest at the smallest of details. He complimented Antimony and the workers on their efforts, smiling and waving at those they passed.

"Can… can I ask a question?" Antimony asked hesitantly.

"Of course. Anything."

"If you were watching Presadia through the mirrors – if you could travel around – why didn't you come back sooner? Presadia needed you, and yet… well, it's as if you didn't care."

"Just because you couldn't see me doesn't mean I was absent. I am king of Presadia, whether those who live here recognize that fact or not. I never ceased to be king, even when others wanted to take the kingship for themselves. A king never stops caring for his people. But this kingdom thought it could do better without me.

"I have always wanted my people to choose to follow me. When my followers – including Kalithor, the one you call the Usurper – turned against me and plotted to overthrow me, when they took power for themselves, they introduced a discord, a not-rightness, that Presadia was never supposed to experience.

"They did it out of selfishness. When people are driven by selfishness, the entire world is affected. It stops others having what they need. When they seize control and power for themselves, others are trodden down and enslaved. When they treat others as objects, people are used and cast aside like rubbish.

"Presadia's cracks are far deeper and more serious than any broken mirror. But just as you cared enough to fix what looked broken beyond repair, so I care enough about Presadia to consider her worth the effort and cost to restore. It grieves my heart to see my beautiful kingdom so fractured and broken. The cracks will forever be a part of this kingdom's history, but perhaps in time people will look back at the cracks and see not the brokenness, but the restoration. They will see not the selfishness, violence and hate that caused the cracks, but the sacrifice, grace and love required to fix them."

They walked for a moment in silence while Antimony considered what the king had said. He had never thought about how broken Presadia was and what it would take to repair all that damage; he had been so caught up with how broken *he* felt.

It was as if the king read Antimony's mind.

"You might feel broken at the moment too, Antimony. You might feel as if who you are, where you have come from, and where you belong are separate pieces of a fractured puzzle. But I hope that one day you too will look back and see that the brokenness from which you came only makes the wholeness you now have even more beautiful."

Antimony nodded, not trusting himself to speak.

Finally, they reached the door to the keep. Antimony ushered the king inside.

"The elves still have a lot of work to do to grow the Great Silvers back to where they used to be. I'm afraid the throne room is rather simple at the moment."

"I am not proud, Antimony. I've lived in rags and poverty for many hundreds of years. I think I can manage."

They entered the throne room. It was packed to bursting with elves, dwarves, and humans. Over by the twisted windows Antimony could see others peering in, including the huge reptilian eyes of the dragons, who didn't want to miss out. A mighty cheer erupted as the king entered, amplified by those outside who couldn't fit into the throne room.

The king turned to Antimony with a slight flick of an eyebrow and a half-smile, an echo of the mysterious stranger Antimony had met in the castle ruins. Then he turned to wave and smile at his cheering subjects. He walked to the centre of the room, reaching out to touch the hands of his people. Eventually, he reached his throne.

It was an old log, the one he had sat on the night Antimony had met him in the Deepwood. Antimony and his friends had brought it back from the forest. Nothing about its physical appearance was any different, but as the king sat himself down it became a throne.

There was a king in Presadia once more.